THE WAY THE WIND BLOWS

Cowgirls in Time Romance Series

A Chill Wind

Wind Beneath My Wings

Against the Wind

The Healing Wind

Ride Like the Wind

Wind of Change

The Way the Wind Blows

THE WAY THE WIND BLOWS

Erica Einhorn

Ralston Store Publishing
P.O. Box 1684
Prescott, Arizona 86302

ISBN 978-1-938322-30-3

Professionally and lovingly edited by:
Jennifer Hope
www.MesaVerdeMediaServices.com

Printed in the USA.

Dedicated to the one I love . . .

CHAPTER ONE

LINDY WAS DUSTING the table by the window when she saw the school bus stop in front of the house. After opening the front door, she stood on the edge of the porch to wait for Cody. When he stepped off the bus, he looked up, saw her, and smiled. Then he ran up the walk and jumped into her arms. She turned him around and around and kissed him on the forehead.

"How was school today, sweetie?" she asked, as she carried him inside the house.

"Good, Mom. I had fun today."

She put him down, and he ran straight for the block castle that he had been constructing that morning. It was an amazing piece of work—especially for a six-year-old —two feet across, a foot high, and he still wasn't finished yet. He looked up at her and smiled, and her heart melted.

It wasn't that long ago that Cody never smiled. Neither of them did. It had been a long journey since the day that she had ended up in the hospital with a broken arm and several broken ribs. Fortunately, besides some bumps and bruises, Cody had not been injured in that incident, but the emotional scars went deep enough. After months of therapy—for both of them—she and Cody were finally on the other side of the whole ordeal.

And now, after Ray, her ex-husband, had been out of prison for a month and had not shown up, she was finally able to breathe easier again. His previous jailhouse experiences always ended with him coming to the house the second that he had been released. Of course, back then, she always took him back. But when she was lying in that hospital bed, and it hurt to breathe through the broken ribs, she finally realized that she didn't deserve to be treated like that. And Cody didn't, either.

Lindy nodded her head, closed her eyes, and smiled. No, if he was going to show up, he would have done it already. They were finally safe from him. And now, for the first time since her divorce, she could start thinking about maybe dating again. What would it be like being around a man who was *kind* to her and kind to Cody? She couldn't even imagine, but she knew that's what she wanted. Someone kind, who treated her and Cody well, someone who took care of and kept them safe, not someone from whom they needed to be kept safe. There *were* men like that out there, and now that everything had settled down in her life, it was time to find one. Maybe she would even marry again. Opening her eyes, she glanced over at Cody still building onto his castle. A good man who would be a good father to Cody—Cody could use a good role model. She didn't want him going through life thinking that all men were as malevolent as his father.

"Cody, come here."

He looked up and said, "I'm in the middle of my *castle*, Mom!"

"C'mon, please. I need a hug."

Cody nodded, smiled, put one more block on the castle, hopped up, and ran over to her. "I love you, Mommy."

She wrapped her arms around him and whispered, "I love you, too, Cody. I'm so lucky to have you."

He pulled away enough so that he could look into her eyes. "I'm lucky to have you, too, Mom! But can I go back to my castle now?"

After another quick kiss on his forehead, she laughed and opened her arms. He collapsed on the floor next to his castle, and immediately started building again. While she watched, she shook her head and smiled. She knew how lucky she was to have him. Cody was such a good boy.

As she watched him, her mind drifted again to starting to date, and she wondered about the man whom she would find attractive. What would she look for? Handsome would be good. As she thought about hair and eye color, what he would do for a living, and how tall he was, she suddenly stopped. Her friends who tried to be very specific about what they were looking for—blond hair and blue eyed, six feet four, banker—were all still unhappily single. No, she would imagine a kind man who treated her and Cody well. A man she could marry and live happily ever after with. Not a perfect man, but perfect for her. Then the doorbell rang. Lindy walked to the door with a smile on her face wondering if it was *him*.

CHAPTER TWO

BRIAN LOOKED OUT the window of the coach, but it was too dark to see anything except blurry shapes. Willie, his oldest, had been looking out the window, but now he was sleeping with his head against the window. Archie, his younger son, had fallen asleep with his head on Brian's shoulder. In the dim moonlight, he could barely see the passengers sitting across from him, but he could still make out his mother, Eliza, his father, Samuel, and between them, little Amy. All three of them were fast asleep. With the gentle swaying motion of the stagecoach, it was difficult not to fall asleep, but Brian had too much to think about for sleep.

Brian *McKenna*. The name still felt awkward to him, but he did remember a time when it felt comfortable. After all, he was born with it. But for the last nine years, he had been Brian Markham. Brian was the name on his shirt when he had been found. The part where his last name had been was missing.

And when he woke up in the Markham's home, with a bandage around his head, and every muscle in his body aching, he didn't know who he was. James Markham, a widower, and his daughter, Bella, had taken care of him for months until he mended enough to do some light work around the farm. By the time he had recovered fully, he and Bella had fallen in love. They married, and a year later she had William. After Willie was born, it took her months to gain her strength back. Bella's constitution was never very strong, and having the baby took a lot out of her. The first year of Willie's life, Brian had to take care of him, because Bella was too weak to leave her bed.

After she felt healthy again, she got pregnant with Archie. When he was born, Bella remained healthy, and everyone thought she had gotten over her weak constitution. But Amy had been born less than a year later, which took even more out of Bella. When the flu swept through town shortly after that, Bella was the first to die. Her father died shortly after, and Brian was left to take care of the children on his own. Both Amy and Archie had gotten sick, but recovered quickly. Brian had been sick briefly, but willed himself to get well, because there was no one left to care for the children. They all recovered—physically—but emotionally, their mother's death had left an empty place in their hearts that one busy parent couldn't fill.

But they made do, and life went on, with him tilling the fields and taking care of the children, schooling them when he had the chance, and leaving much too much work and responsibility to Willie, who had to be grown up before his time. Years passed, the war ended, and the children grew. Sometimes he'd look at them and wonder where the time went. And then one day, a wagon pulled up in front of the house. Willie had come out to the field to tell him that they were looking for Brian McKenna.

Brian had walked out to the wagon to tell them there was no McKenna here, but when he saw them, he immediately knew who they were. Mama and Papa, who had come all the way from Colorado Territory to find him.

It was a teary reunion, with Mama crying and holding him so tightly that he couldn't move, and Papa alternately patting him on the shoulder and shaking his hand. Brian blinked back tears remembering how it had all happened and looked at Mama and Papa now sitting across from him, sleeping.

They had stayed at the farm for a few days catching up and then they packed up the house, and started the long journey west. Now the journey was almost done. He had lost track, but he thought they'd be home in a day or two. Home. It had been so many years that he hardly remembered what Red Bluff was like. He had been a kid himself when he left there to fight in the Civil War.

Papa said that a lot of new people—good people— had moved into town. And then Mama had given him a funny look. It was the same look she had on her face when Brian asked how they knew he was still alive and living in Virginia. No matter how many times he had asked, Mama and Papa would look at each other, raise their eyebrows, and shrug their shoulders. One time, when they thought he was sleeping, he had overheard them having a conversation about "telling" him something. Unfortunately, that something was still elusive, and he had no idea how they had found him, or even how they figured out that he was alive, since he had been reported dead.

Regardless, he was happy to be alive and happy that they had found him. Now the children had grandparents, and although he would be "new" to town, he could finally think about settling down again. Meeting a woman. Getting married. Have a mother for his children, and have someone to come home to at night. He would like that. And it would be so good for the children to have a mother again. Not that anyone could take Bella's place, either in his heart or theirs, but someone that nonetheless, they could all love. He wondered if that was in his future.

Although it didn't sound like there were many single women in town. But they said that you never knew, because new people were coming in all the time. When he had asked where they were coming from, Mama and Papa gave him that look again and changed the subject. But he hoped there was someone out there for him. Someone to make his family complete. And he had the feeling that life was going to get really good for him in Red Bluff. He felt like something good was about to come his way. Not that he wasn't already grateful for everything that had happened to him in the last couple of months, but that didn't mean that more good things couldn't come his way. And he had a feeling they *were* coming his way. And he couldn't wait.

CHAPTER THREE

WHEN LINDY HAD opened the door with a smile on her face, she had never expected to see Ray standing there. She didn't even have time for her smile to droop, though, because Ray had said, "I'm going to wipe that smile off your face," and then he hit her in the mouth.

Ten minutes later, cowering in the corner, trying to shield Cody, and with blood dripping from her cut lip, she heard a siren in the distance. Ray had stopped hitting her, and she saw a fleeting look of panic on his face, before he rushed out the front door, leaving it open. He turned once, scowled, and said, "I'll be back to finish what I started. And I'm taking *him* with me." After pointing at Cody, he disappeared.

Her neighbor, Sandra—the one who had called the police—came in the front door and ran over to her and Cody. "Are you all right? I called the police as soon as I heard the screams, but I was afraid it wasn't soon enough. Are you okay?" Sandra helped Lindy up, but it was difficult, because Cody wouldn't let go of her and was weighing her down.

"I think we're both okay." She felt her ribs, put weight

on both legs separately, and stretched out her arms. Then she wiped her hand across her mouth. "I think this is the worst of it. Nothing broken. And he pushed Cody down, but didn't hit him or kick him."

"Are you sure you're all right?"

Lindy leaned down, felt her legs, and winced. "I think I'll be black and blue tomorrow, but nothing serious." She hugged Cody to her and whispered, "We're fine, Cody. We're both fine. It's going to be all right."

"I didn't think he was coming back, Mommy."

"I didn't think so, either, Cody. But we're all right. Sandra called the police, and we're safe now."

"You're so calm about this!" Sandra slowly shook her head. "I'd be hysterical."

"I have to be strong for the next few minutes, and then I'm sure I'll get hysterical." The sirens had gotten increasingly louder, and glancing out the window, Lindy saw that they had stopped in front of the house. She watched as the policemen jumped out of the car, but approached the house cautiously. Stepping out the door, she waved to them. "It's okay. He heard the siren and left. He's gone now."

The police walked over to her. The older one, with a look of concern on his face, glanced at her lip and said, "That looks awfully bad, Ma'am. You better have it looked at." Then he straightened up and took out a pad of paper. "You do want to press charges, don't you?"

Lindy shook her head. "No, I don't."

Sandra stepped up from behind her. "Lindy! You have to! He'll come back!"

"Ma'am, victims of domestic abuse who take back their partners, usually suffer that abuse again." The policeman gently shook the pad of paper like he wanted her to get on with it. "Come on. It's the only way to stop the cycle."

"No. The only way to stop this cycle is for me to go so far away that he'll never find me. And that's where I'm going." She put her hand out to the older policeman and touched him on the arm. "Don't worry. I'm not going back to the jerk. I learned that lesson when he put me in the hospital."

The policeman put the paper back in his pocket. "I'm glad to hear it. Some women never learn, and then we have to deal with a homicide."

"I think a homicide is what he had in mind if you hadn't come when you did. So thank you. And I think we better go now before he gets the idea to come back."

"Will you be leaving right now, Ma'am?"

"As soon as I pack some clothes."

"Would you like us to wait in case he comes back?"

Lindy tilted her head and smiled at him—and it hurt. "Oh, that would be great. I won't be long. Thanks! Come on, Cody." She stepped into the house, followed by Sandra.

"Where are you going? You know if you go to your mother's, he'll know."

"No, I'm not going there. It would cost a fortune to get a ticket that left today. I have another place in mind. A place where he'll never find us."

"Where?" asked Sandra.

Lindy looked at her and shrugged. "I don't know! A friend of mine lives *there*, but she wouldn't tell me where it is. Just that it's in a place where we'd be safe from Ray." Lindy threw a handful of Cody's clothes into a backpack and then filled a small duffle bag with some of her clothes. "This is all we'll take. We'll figure everything out later. I just want to get out of here." She walked out the door with Cody still hanging on her. Sandra followed them out.

"Will you let me know when you get there safe?" Sandra put her arm on Lindy's shoulder. "I worry about you, you know."

"That's the thing. There's no phone and no mail where I'm going. Just remember, Sandra. No news is good news. If anything bad happens, you'll hear about it on the news!"

CHAPTER FOUR

THEY HAD ARRIVED in town late in the evening, and Brian had hardly gotten any sleep at all. Now they were finishing breakfast while Samuel walked over to the telegraph office. He would send the telegram today, and tomorrow someone would pick them up. Only one more night in a hotel, fortunately. And then they would be home.

"Brian, you must be looking forward to getting home," said Eliza.

"Ma, I hate to disappoint you"—she already looked disappointed which made him feel bad—"but it really isn't home to me. I barely remember it, and you know, William and I left less than two years after we moved there." That made Ma look even worse. Any mention of her dead son William made her all-overish.

"Yes, I suppose you're right, Brian. But your father and I have lived there many years now, and it's home for us." She reached out and patted his hand. "And soon it will feel like home to you, too."

"It will feel like home after the children and I have a place of our own." He glanced at the children. "And it will take me a while to save up enough money to arrange that."

"We told you, Brian. Money isn't a problem anymore."

"Ma! Yes, you've said that, but you've never explained it, and until I understand why money isn't a problem, I have to think that it is. I'm poor as Job's turkey! And I know that you and Pa aren't rich. So, tell me!" he pleaded.

Eliza looked at Brian and nodded. As she was about to open her mouth, she looked at the children sitting at the table staring at her. "The children. I can't say it in front of the children."

Brian exhaled quickly in frustration. "Children, please wait for your grandfather over there by the door. Don't get in the way, though." Willie, the oldest, ushered the children away from the table. Brian waited until they were out of hearing range. "All right? Now tell me!"

Eliza leaned forward. "It all started when—"

Samuel walked up to the table with the children hanging on his arms. "What's this I hear that the children aren't welcome at the table? Well, that's a fine state of affairs!" He held the chairs out for each child to sit down. "Now what's going on?"

"I was about to tell Brian—"

"We discussed this, Eliza. And we decided—" Samuel said, with knitted brows and a scowl on his face.

"Pa, this isn't fair! You're keeping something from me, and I don't like it!"

Eliza patted Brian's arm and looked at him sympathetically. Then, to her husband, she said, "Samuel, did you send the telegram?"

"No. I did not!"

"What do you mean, you didn't? How will we get home?"

Samuel smiled and held up six tickets in his hand. "We're taking the stage!"

"To Red Bluff? There's a stage to Red Bluff now?" asked Eliza.

"Yes, and we'll be on it in an hour!" Samuel smiled.

"Did you still send a telegram so they know we're coming?"

"No, Eliza, I thought it would be better as a surprise." Samuel reached across the table and put his hand on Brian's arm. "And once you get settled in, we can start looking for a place for you."

Brian felt frustrated. "Pa, I know you keep saying that, but I'm not able to buy a house right now."

"We told you, Brian. Money is not a problem."

Brian shook his head. He felt tired and grumpy, and he now pushed away from the table and stood up. "Until you tell me how you have an endless supply of money, I have to think that it *is* a problem. Tell me when the stage gets here. Until then, I'll be in the room."

He stomped away from the table and climbed the stairs two at a time. After closing the door quietly—it wasn't his house to slam the door—he flung himself on the bed. He was a grown man with children of his own! Why were they treating him like a child? What could be so secret that they couldn't tell him? Had they found a gold mine or something?

Turning over on his back, he stared at the tin ceiling. Regardless of where the money came from, it *would* be good to have his own place without worrying about saving up to buy it. And his *own* place—even though he worked James Markham's farm after James died, it never felt like *his*. It felt like he was working it for somebody else.

A small ranch with some horses, maybe run a few cows—he nodded his head—yeah, that would be good. If he could let go of the need to know where the money came from and that his parents were keeping secrets from him, he could enjoy the benefits of that money, and he and his children would be better for it. It was his choice to be upset about it or not. At that moment, he decided that he was not going to let it upset him any longer. Sighing, he sat up in bed as Willie opened the door and announced, "Papa! The stage is here! Let's go home!"

CHAPTER FIVE

AFTER SANDRA LEFT, Lindy looked around the room at the damage that Ray had caused. Cody's castle was completely demolished, with blocks strewn all over the floor. A table and the lamp that sat atop it were knocked over onto the floor. Lindy sighed, picked up the backpack and the duffle bag, grabbed Cody's hand, and started for the door.

Cody broke away, dashed up the stairs, and called out, "Wait!" He came back downstairs holding his toy dachshund. It was a raggedy thing that Cody had had for years. It was reddish brown with shiny black button eyes. Cody loved it.

They walked out the front door and down the walk toward the police car. Now that her adrenalin had calmed down, her bruised legs had started to bother her, causing her to limp. "Thank you again, officers. I appreciate you getting here so quickly."

"Ma'am, are you sure you don't need to go to the hospital?" He nodded toward her limp and her lip.

"No, just bad bruises. No broken bones."

"Would you like us to follow you where you're going?

Make sure you get there safe?"

"No, thank you. Ray looked panicked when he heard the siren. I don't think he'd be hanging around anywhere."

"If he gives you any more trouble, Ma'am, please don't hesitate to call." The two policemen stepped over to the doors of their car.

"Thank you for everything." Lindy waved at them and smiled, though that made her lip hurt.

She helped Cody into the car, strapped on the seatbelt, and then got in herself. Her emotions felt like they were about to erupt. When she drove off, the police followed for a couple of blocks and then turned off. Although she would have liked not to break down in front of Cody, she had her limits. And with that thought, the tears started pouring out of her eyes, and her chest heaved in great sobs.

Cody reached over and patted her arm. "It's okay, Mommy. It's okay. We're safe now. He can't hurt us now." After hesitating for minute, he asked, "Can he?"

Lindy tried to catch her breath. "No, Cody. We're going where he'll never find us and can't get to us. We'll be safe there."

"Okay, Mommy." He pulled his hand away and stuck his thumb in his mouth.

When Lindy saw that, she winced. He hadn't done that since the last time Ray had abused them. Oh, well. There was nothing she could do about it now. It's over and done, and they were going to safety. She didn't know where that was, but she knew the first step was driving over to Rachel's friend, Madison's. Rachel, a friend of hers who had "disappeared" a year ago, told her that if she ever needed to get away, that she should go to Madison's ranch, and Madison would help her. So that's where they were headed now. It took her a while to find the ranch because she wasn't exactly sure where it was. But after turning on one street after another, she found it.

Lindy pulled up in front of the house and noticed all the cars parked in the back. There was a truck and a car in the driveway close to the house. She parked out of the way by the cars in the back and noticed that Rachel's car was among them. Where they were going didn't require a car? If she had to buy plane tickets, she'd have to put them on her credit card and worry about it later. After pulling the backpack and duffle from the car, she stepped around the other side and opened the door for Cody. His thumb was still in his mouth, and he looked around dreamily. "Come on, let's go, Cody."

He got out and took her hand while still clutching the stuffed dachshund, and then they walked to the front door. Exhaling quickly, she knocked on the door. When a young woman answered and raised her eyebrows with a questioning look, Lindy said, "Madison? I'm Lindy. Remember we talked on the phone when I was looking for Rachel?"

"Oh, Lindy! Come in! I should have recognized you"—she pointed to Rachel's lip which had grown larger since the attack—"Rachel told me that you might come if you needed to get away."

"We definitely need to get away. As soon as possible. I don't think Ray followed me here, but if nothing else, he's very determined."

"We can take you first thing tomorrow morning. Would that be soon enough?"

"Oh, Madison, I'm so afraid to wait." Tears started

18

running down her face.

Madison looked at her with compassion and squeezed her arm. "It's late, but I suppose Zack can take you this afternoon, if you leave right away." She stepped into the hallway and called out, "Zack! Can you come here, please?"

"I'll be right there," called Zack.

A minute later, Zack walked out from the hallway. An attractive man with dark hair and dark eyes, he smiled when he saw her. "Hi, I'm Zack."

"Oh, sorry!" said Madison. "Lindy, this is my boyfriend, Zack." She looked at Zack with concern. "Zack, do you think you can ride Lindy and her son over to the old Red Bluff?"

"I'm Cody," Cody said and held out his hand to shake Zack's. The dachshund fell to the floor, but nobody noticed.

"Today? It's getting pretty late."

Lindy could feel the tears running down her face again, but she didn't say anything. She stood there biting her already sore lip to keep from bursting out in sobs.

"Zack, she's afraid her ex will come for her. She wants to get out *as soon as*. See what he already did?"

Zack looked at Lindy's lip and the tears on her face. "Oh, yeah, wow. Yeah, let's go. But, Madison, I'm not leaving you here if he could show up."

"I'll be fine," said Madison.

"That's what *I* thought." Lindy sniffled.

"You're coming with me, Madison. I mean it."

Madison nodded. "Okay, let's get going."

19

CHAPTER SIX

BEFORE BRIAN EVER stepped into the stagecoach, he had decided that he wasn't going to sulk about Ma and Pa keeping secrets from him. They'd tell him when they told him, and that was that. If they had a fortune in gold stashed somewhere, then so be it. He'd accept any gifts graciously. After all, he had to think about the children, too. And having their own house would be good for them—and what they were used to.

Shifting his weight yet again, he tried to get comfortable. Two other people had bought stage tickets before Pa bought theirs, so they either had to wait for another day, or try to squeeze in. When it didn't look like it was going to work at all, the driver suggested that Willie ride up top with him. Ma was worried, but Willie really wanted to, so Brian had let him. He didn't think he had seen a smile so big on Willie's face since before his mother had died.

Amy jumped up from her grandfather's lap and moved over to Brian. "Papa, it's your turn!" Then she jumped onto his lap.

Brian nodded and put his arms around her. It would

be good for Amy to have a mother. She had been so long without. The boys had, too, but it didn't seem as hard on them. A girl needed a woman. Yes, Amy now had Eliza, but still, a mother of her own would be of great benefit to her. It would do him good, too. He hadn't even thought about another woman for so many years. Now, away from the workload and responsibility of the farm, it was something that he could think about. Something he could desire. And for some reason, that desire was growing. It was like he hadn't thought of it for so long and now that he was thinking about it, he wanted her *now*. A woman in his life. Yes, he wanted her now.

Amy leaned against him and was soon asleep. The swaying of the coach and her even breathing got to him, and he fell asleep, too. It was a few hours later when Archie shook him by the arm.

"Papa! Papa! Grandda says we're almost there! We're almost there!"

Amy yawned, stood up in the close quarters, and climbed onto her grandmother's lap. Brian stretched and looked out the window. There was a ranch there—a small place, with a barn and a fenced pasture. It was a little small for his family, but that's what he wanted. A place like that, only bigger. And he smiled. It was a smile that had come from deep inside him and gave him a feeling of satisfaction all over his body. It felt like—home. And although he had felt a little apprehension on moving his family back to a place where he had hardly spent any time, he now felt like he was bringing them home. He glanced at Ma, holding Amy on her lap, and at Pa, who was talking with Archie, and he felt like this was exactly where he was supposed to be. And he also felt, curiously enough, that he would find a mother for Amy and the boys—a wife for him.

Then, a few feet off the road, two riders emerged from between two thick bushes. A woman with long, dark hair with a young blond boy riding behind her, and on the other horse a dark man with a blonde woman riding behind him. The dark man and dark woman looked like they belonged together, but the blonde woman and the boy not only looked separate, but they looked alone and lost in the world. It was a feeling that he had had more than once since Bella died. Yes, the children were there for him, always, but he still felt alone at times. He felt compassion for the blonde woman and had a strange urge to want to hold her in his arms and comfort her.

Then the stagecoach was past them and even trying to look back out the window proved futile. The smile remained on his face, though, and broadened when he saw the sign for Red Bluff.

A few more minutes and they were in town—and a surprise celebration. People lined the streets, and there was a big banner stretched between the hotel on one side of the street and the saloon on the other. The sign read: Welcome home, Brian McKenna!

"Pa? I thought you never sent a telegram that we were arriving today."

Pa shrugged. "I didn't, Brian. I don't know how they knew."

When they stepped out of the stagecoach, Brian's grandda ran up to hug him. "Brian! Brian!" He wouldn't let him go, just stared into his face. "We thought you were gone, boy. We thought you were gone." When tears started in his eyes, he gave Brian one more quick hug, found Eliza and Samuel, hugged them, and then walked back into the hotel.

People started hugging Ma and Pa, but Brian didn't recognize any of them. There was one woman who hugged Ma, and he heard Ma say to her, "Thank you. Thank you for bringing back my boy." And then Ma started crying while the woman patted her on the back. Whatever did that mean? And who was the woman?

CHAPTER SEVEN

LINDY DIDN'T BELIEVE them until they came out of the cave and she saw the stagecoach. Drawing in a deep breath, she said, "You weren't kidding! Cody, look at that!" A man sitting at the window in the stagecoach looked at her like he knew her. It wasn't a look of recognition really, it was more like he had looked into her soul and knew what was there. Of course it wouldn't be recognition—this was now the nineteenth century!

She thought back to the last thirty minutes. It had started when Zack and Madison were ready, and they all walked out to the barn. "What are we doing here?" she had asked.

"We're going to where you're safe. We'll take you to Rachel." Madison started brushing and saddling her horse.

"On horseback? We're going on horseback?" Lindy still couldn't believe it, but Cody was jumping up and down with excitement.

"I get to ride a horse! I get to ride a horse!"

They rode along the trail, with Lindy sitting behind Zack, a little uncomfortable because they were riding bareback, without a saddle, so her arms were tight around his waist, and Cody sitting behind Madison, who was in a saddle. And then Zack and Madison started telling her a story that sounded so far-fetched that she could hardly believe it. A tale of a cave that was a time-travel portal to the nineteenth century—a place with no cell phones, no electricity, and no bathrooms—only outhouses. And although she knew that Rachel had said that no one could reach her by mail or telephone, it was too much for Lindy to believe.

When they had gone through the cave, she didn't feel any different, and she expected to *feel* different in the nineteenth century. So until she saw the stagecoach, with the four black horses, she hadn't believed. "Then it's real."

"We wouldn't kid you about something like this," said Madison. "We're almost there now. See, there's the sign for Red Bluff. But I think we should wait here a minute while the dust settles from the stagecoach."

They had ridden out onto the main—dirt—road, and particles of dust filled the air. "Red Bluff? I don't understand."

"This is the Red Bluff from over a hundred years ago. See the mountains over there?" Zack shifted and turned his head to speak to her.

"Wow! I can't believe it! Oh! And the sign!"

They stayed at the side of the road while the dust settled. Lindy looked around. Trees and bushes everywhere. And the road not only was dirt, but it was narrow and had wagon ruts.

"You know Jenna, right?" Madison looked at her, with Cody behind her, still all smiles.

"Sure, I know Jenna."

"Jenna is the one who found it—accidentally. She got caught in a snowstorm and took shelter in the cave. When she came out the other side, she wandered into town. Now she's married to the sheriff, and they just had a baby!"

Lindy shook her head. "Unbelievable."

"And her sister, Kat? She lives here, too, married to the town doctor. Do you know Sarah? She married the saloon keeper, and now she sings in the saloon! You must know Ryan, right? He bought the general store, and he's married now, too."

"And it's so close. All this and so close, too. I still can't believe it."

"Okay, let's go on." Zack moved his horse down the road. "Madison, we need to get back before dark."

The horses proceeded down the dirt road, and several minutes later, they came to the town. Lindy couldn't believe it. A bank, general store, hotel, saloon, sheriff's office—like an old west town. "It looks like a movie set! And look, a celebration—for Brian. Who's Brian?"

Madison and Zack turned their horses to avoid the crowded celebratory main street. "Jenna thought it was a movie set, too, until she saw a gunfight where a guy got killed," said Madison. "The celebration is because Eliza and Samuel—they own the hotel—found out that their son, Brian, whom they thought had been killed in the Civil War, was really alive. They went back east to get him, and they must have just returned."

Zack turned his head to talk to her. "And guess how they found out he was alive? Jenna found it on the internet! How cool is that!"

"Wow," said Lindy thoughtfully. "So all those people moved here and have better lives, and they helped the people who already live here have better lives. It sounds like win-win to me. It looks like a wonderful place, and I know we'll be happy here. But honestly, all I care about now is that we're safe from Ray."

"Oh, you're safe all right. He would never think of looking in the past for you!" Madison pointed up ahead. "There's Rachel's house right there."

They rode up to the house. Lindy slid off Zack's horse; Zack got off and helped Cody down. Then he helped her carry the duffle to the front door. "We'll stay to make sure she's home." He knocked on the door, while Lindy and Cody stood by expectantly.

"Thanks so much, Zack and Madison. I appreciate your riding me over here—and explaining everything."

The door opened and Rachel stood there with her mouth open. Then she closed it and said, "I see Ray paid you a visit again." She pointed at Lindy's mouth, and Lindy nodded. "Come on in! Thanks Madison and Zack for bringing her!"

CHAPTER EIGHT

WHEN RAY SAW Lindy's car go by followed by the cops, he stiffened. But she didn't see him, and they didn't look like they were searching for him. He pulled to the corner, waited until he saw the cops turn off, and then he followed her from a respectable distance behind. She didn't drive like she knew where she was going—she kept turning this way and that way, which made it difficult to follow her. Then she disappeared. He couldn't find her anywhere. Ray felt himself getting angrier and angrier, and his hands balled up into fists of their own accord. It took him forty-five minutes and a lucky turn to spot her car.

The house wasn't anyplace like he expected her to go. It looked like a small ranch, complete with a barn. There were many cars parked outside toward the back, and her car was one of them. Two other cars were parked close to the door of the house. Although it looked like everyone was home, there was no movement inside, but he wanted to wait to be sure.

Lighting a cigarette while he waited, his fingers drummed the dashboard harder and harder until he was hitting it with his fist. That woman made him so mad that he wanted to pulverize her! And then, when she was lying there weak and vulnerable, he would give the kid a good kick in front of her, and then haul him off. It wasn't that he wanted the kid; he didn't. Ray never believed it was his kid, anyway. He wanted to push Lindy as far as he could. Taking the kid would do that.

After tossing the cigarette out the window, he slowly got out of the car and closed the door as quietly as possible. Approaching the house from the side, he quickly glanced in the window and saw no movement. Moving to the next window and the next, he found no movement at all. Feeling more confident now, he strode to the front door and rang the doorbell. When no one answered he rang again and began pounding on the door. No answer. When he tried the door knob and it turned in his hand, he smiled and walked in like he owned the place.

Looking around, the first thing that he saw was the stuffed dachshund. Yeah, they were here. It made him angry all over again. At first he stooped to pick it up, then thought better of it and kicked it out to the middle of the room. He jumped up and down on it, making angry grunting noises. Then he picked it up, hit it in the face with his fist, and looked around. He stomped into the kitchen, looked around again, until he spotted the knives. Picking out a cleaver, he put the dachshund on the cutting board—he thought that was appropriate— and cut its head off. Leaving the cleaver on the counter, he took both pieces and threw them down where he had first found it. But he still felt really angry, so he kicked over some tables, walked out the front door, and slammed it behind him as hard as he could.

Where was she? Where would that blasted woman go

and take his kid with her? If he was his kid, probably not. When he noticed the barn, he walked toward it. Stepping inside, he found no horses, but saw the fresh droppings. She went horseback riding? I didn't even know she knew how to ride a horse, he thought. I beat her up good, and what does she do but go horseback riding. It didn't make sense to him. Since no one was around, he walked out the side door of the barn to a corral with a gate on the other side of it. He followed the hoof prints out through another gate and ended up on the public property behind the ranch. There was no way he could follow the tracks out here. There was no telling how far they might have gone. If he had a motorbike or a bicycle he could follow them.

But not now. Glancing down at his watch, next to his prison tattoo, he realized that he was almost late to see his parole officer. Couldn't keep the man waiting now, could we? After walking back to his car and getting in, he drove to the office. When he ran his fingers through his hair, he noticed some blood on his sleeve. Her blood. Should he wash it off or something? No time. He'd tell the stupid jerk that he had gotten a bloody nose. Yeah, that would work.

CHAPTER NINE

BRIAN LOOKED AROUND at all the decorations and heard the sound of food preparations in the restaurant kitchen. "Ma, I didn't want to make a big deal out of this. I wanted us to blend in so nobody would notice us."

"Oh, Brian dear, I'm so happy you're home, and I wanted to share our happiness with the whole town."

"The whole town? That sounds expensive." Brian shook his head as he looked around. Ma gave him a look, so he dropped it.

"Besides, we have some wonderful new friends that I want you to meet." Eliza put her hand on his arm and looked at him lovingly.

"Oh, Ma."

As Ma walked out of the room, Pa came in and put his hand on Brian's shoulder. "Son, this party would make your mother very happy. Just let her do it. It will be fine. The children love it."

"All right, Pa. All right. Is there anything I can do to help?" The children were in the kitchen with "Granny," the woman that his grandfather had married while Brian was back east.

"You're the guest of honor! No, just relax and enjoy life!"

Brian exhaled slowly and nodded his head. He didn't want to go back to their room—the four of them, he and the three children—shared a big room on the main floor. It had a curious necessary—inside. It was the strangest gadget he had ever seen. But the children loved it— especially Amy, who had once been bitten by a spider in their necessary back home. He moved his head from side to side. No, not back home. *This* was home now. And although their cramped quarters didn't feel like home, he knew that eventually they would have their own roomy place.

Opening the front door of the hotel, he stepped out and surveyed the town. Smiling with anticipation, he walked up the street past the bank and the general store, turned the corner, and the next corner, and walked back down the street. When he got to the livery, he stopped. There was a man out front talking to someone about a wagon, so he approached him. "Is it all right if I go in and look at the horses?"

"Sure. If you see one you want to rent, let me know. The ones on the end back there are all privately owned."

Brian nodded, walked inside, and inhaled the pleasant scent of horses and leather. He had horses back in Virginia—a couple plow horses for the fields, and one riding horse—but it was James Markham's horse, and still felt like it was Markham's horse even after the old man had died. Walking down past the stalls, he looked at each horse and petted the ones that came to the gate, which was most of them. Good. They were well treated, then. The worst thing was people mistreating animals or children.

When he got to the last stalls, he looked at the private horses and smiled. He wanted a horse of his own, and as he turned around and saw the small horse on the other side, he thought he'd like to have a couple of small ones for Amy and Archie, and a bigger one for Willie. They'd like that. And that made him wonder if there was enough money for him to buy or build himself a house, then perhaps there would be enough money to buy some horses. With those thoughts, the idea of a stash of gold didn't bother him so much.

He didn't know how long he spent in there talking to and petting the horses, but the men in front were still talking when he left. Waving to them, he said "thank you" and walked up the street. When he came to the intersection, he saw a school on one corner, a house across from it, and to his left was a doctor's office. The building across from that looked empty. Turning the corner and walking up the street, he glanced into the saloon, but there was a sign on the door that said, "Closed! Come to the party across the street!" And there was no one inside.

Straightening up and preparing himself for what lay ahead, he walked into the hotel to a room full of people. They were in the entryway and more of them in the restaurant. He stood there, not knowing which way to turn, when Ma came up to him.

"Brian! We've been looking all over for you!" She looked at the couple standing with her, the woman was holding a baby, and the man wore a sheriff's badge. "This is Josiah, the sheriff, his wife, Jenna, and their baby, Milo. And this is my son, Brian."

Then Ma unexpectedly broke down in tears and hugged Jenna. He heard her whisper "thank you" into

Jenna's ear and then slip away. It was the same woman she had thanked earlier. What was that about? "Nice meeting you, Josiah." Brian shook his hand. "Hallo, Jenna and Milo!"

"We understand that you and your children are staying in our old quarters." Josiah nodded behind him toward where Brian's room was.

"Yeah, it's a little crowded, but it's fine until I can find my own place." Brian nodded.

"Well, we were talking and since we stayed there while Jenna was pregnant with Milo, we thought it would only be neighborly to offer you our place until you find your own. You'll be more comfortable there. It's got two bedrooms, and one of your kids could sleep on the sofa."

"Oh, no, we couldn't put you out like that!" Brian was astonished at the invitation. He didn't even know these people, and they were making a generous offer.

Jenna looked at Brian. "Brian, we insist. Honestly. We stayed here before, and for the three of us"—she nodded in the direction of the room—"that room has more than enough space. We can make the switch tomorrow. All right? You have to say yes, because we're not going to take no for an answer."

"She's right, Brian. You have to say yes."

Brian shrugged. "All right then. Yes!"

Josiah shook his hand again, and Jenna hugged him. "I'm the one who found you after all," said Jenna.

"You're the one who found me? What do you mean?"

"Oops," said Jenna.

Josiah cleared his throat. "Eliza and Samuel didn't tell you how they found you?"

"No, it was like a big secret. Very annoying."

Josiah's and Jenna's eyes met, and they looked all-overish. "Well, sorry ole boy, then we can't tell you, either. But I'll come by tomorrow with a wagon so we can make the switch." Josiah took Jenna by the arm and led her and the baby away.

Before Brian had a chance to think about what had just happened, Ma came back over leading two men and a woman. "Brian, this is Rachel and Nick, they just got married. Nick is the deputy sheriff. And this is Matthew; he owns the saloon across the street. And this is my son, Brian."

Brian shook the men's hands and nodded to Rachel. "Nice meeting you all. Congratulations on your marriage, Nick and Rachel."

"Thank you."

Matthew pointed across the room. "That's my wife, Sarah, over there standing with Lindy. Sarah's the one with her back to us."

Brian nodded and glanced in the direction that Matthew had pointed. The woman talking to Matthew's wife was the blonde woman that he had seen riding double on the horse. His heart fluttered in his chest. And her name was Lindy.

CHAPTER TEN

LINDY HAD BARELY gotten settled in when Rachel and her husband, Nick, whisked her off to the party at the hotel. Rachel had dressed her in one of her long skirts—women weren't allowed to wear jeans in the nineteenth century—and a pretty blouse. When she had tried to beg off, saying what a long day it had been, they told her that it was a good way to get to meet everyone in town. So she and Cody had followed Nick and Rachel, who were holding hands, and their two boys, Oscar and Jamie, who were holding hands. Both Oscar and Jamie were adopted, but you could tell that they were well-loved. She hoped that some day she could be part of a whole family again.

The party was crowded with people. Not only was the restaurant full, but guests were spilling over into the entryway. Rachel started introducing her to people, but Lindy found that she already knew some of them—by sight, if not by name. She knew Jenna and her friend, Sarah, and she knew of Kat and Ryan—Jenna's brother and sister. But she met all of their spouses—all of them nineteenth century people. The only one who lived here and had married a twenty-first-century person was Rachel. They had both moved to the nineteenth century for jobs—Rachel to be a teacher, and Nick to be the deputy sheriff—and didn't "find" each other for months.

Cody ran off with Jamie and his brother, Oscar, and three other children that Rachel didn't know. But Rachel told Lindy that Cody would be safe with them. Lindy saw Sarah at the dessert table and started talking to her.

"How long have you lived here now, Sarah?"

"Nearly a year. And I've never been happier!"

"Don't you ever miss the conveniences of *there*?" Rachel had told Lindy that they never talk about the twenty-first century unless they're positively alone, so everyone referred to it as *there*.

"Well, I haven't given this up"—Sarah looked around and turned her body so no one could see, and then she pulled out her cell phone—"or *this*." After returning her cell phone to her pocket, she held up a spoonful of Rocky Road Ice Cream.

"Yeah, where'd that come from? I didn't think they had any here." Lindy helped herself to another helping of pie and scooped out some Rocky Road to go with it.

"Ryan. When he heard that Brian was about to arrive —someone had seen them in the next town—he took his wagon over *there* to get all these goodies. Rocky Road ice cream! Neopolitan! Cakes, pies! Ryan thinks of everything!"

"Yeah! It sure looks like it! Where is Brian, the guest of honor?"

"I think that must be him over there. Eliza just introduced him to Matthew and Josiah and Jenna. See Matthew? He's my husband—a real hunk, isn't he?" Sarah nodded her head and smiled as she looked at her husband.

"Yes, he is handsome. And so is Brian! I wonder if he's single." Lindy didn't say anything more, but she realized that he was the man that she had seen go by in the stage-coach. The man she thought had looked into her soul.

Just then, three children, two boys and a girl, sur-rounded him. The little girl kept grabbing at his arm until he picked her up and swung her around, much to the girl's delight.

"Those must be his children," said Sarah.

Disappointed, Lindy said, "Oh. Then he must already be married." That thought made her hurt in her gut. It was odd. She hadn't even met him yet, had only seen him once before, but she already felt a connection to him. But he was married. How utterly and completely disappointing. Lindy's shoulders drooped, and she sighed deeply.

Lindy watched him with his kids, and she liked the way he was with them. He looked like a really loving father—not like Ray. Brian ruffled the older boy's hair and hugged the younger boy. The kids looked up at him like they thought he was a king. Cody had never once looked at Ray that way—not even before the abuse started. As she watched Brian, she had to smile at how kind he looked. She liked kind; she wanted kind.

Suddenly, he picked up his head from kissing one of the boys on the head and looked straight at her. He smiled, put down his daughter, and started walking straight toward her.

"Oh! You have an admirer! He's coming right over to meet you, Lindy!" Sarah put one more bite of pie in her mouth and turned to walk away.

"But, Sarah, he's got children! I'll go ask Jenna and see

if I can find out the scoop for you! Good luck!" Sarah turned and walked away, leaving Lindy standing at the dessert table by herself.

Lindy smiled as he walked up from across the room, and she tried to still her beating heart. She kept telling herself not to get carried away with a man who may already be taken.

Brian came right up to her. "Hi, I'm—"

Lindy nodded. "Brian! And I'm—"

"Lindy," Brian said. They both laughed. "I saw you from the stagecoach," Brian said at the same time Lindy said, "I saw you on the stagecoach!" They both laughed again. Brian reached out, grabbed both her hands, and smiled into her eyes. "We're already finishing each other's sentences, and we just met. I guess that means we should get married!" Brian laughed again, but there was a note of seriousness about what he had said.

The statement made Lindy uncomfortable. She involuntarily slipped out of his grasp and took a step backward. She didn't even know if he was already married—but if he was, would he have said something like that? Besides being an abuser, Ray was a womanizer, and she didn't want any more of that. But wanting to break the awkward moment, she said, "Are those your children who were climbing on you?"

"Yeah, they're blossoming here. You know, we moved here from Virginia, and it's been a hard few years after their mother died." Brian looked at the floor and seemed sad.

"I'm sorry." Lindy put her hand on his arm and squeezed. Then, self-consciously, quickly drew it away.

"It's been a tough few years. My wife and my father-in-law died of the flu a few years ago, and I've been

39

running the farm and taking care of the kids by myself since then." He looked down at the floor again, clenched his mouth, and then brightened. "Then, out of nowhere, my mother and father show up in Virginia and tell me that my name isn't Markham after all—I had been using that name since I got shot in the head in the Civil War and couldn't remember who I was. 'Brian' was on my shirt." He shrugged. "Anyway, I don't know how they found me, but I'm glad they did!"

"Oh, they found you because—" Suddenly, Lindy realized that if he didn't know already, she probably shouldn't be the one to tell him.

"Because—," he encouraged.

Lindy was so flustered, she didn't know what to do. It had been a hard day, emotionally, and she couldn't deal with this. "I have to go now." Abruptly, she started walking away from him, then turned around quickly and said, "Nice meeting you, Brian!"

CHAPTER ELEVEN

BRIAN WAS BEGUNKED. Lindy was about to tell him how his parents had found him, and suddenly she went pale and walked away. Why all the theatrics on how they found him? Had they gone to a gypsy fortuneteller or something? He shook his head. All the secrecy over the money and about how they found him. It was the dangedest thing.

He sure did like her, though. That short blonde hair made her look like a little pixie. And those blue eyes that bore right through him. What a woman! It wasn't just the last comment that had bothered her, though. It was also his comment about finishing each other's sentences. That seemed to scare her, too. Had it been that long since he courted someone that he didn't know what made a woman feel good and what scared her off? Well, he wasn't going to hang up his fiddle on Lindy just yet. He had taken a cotton to her, and he had a feeling that she had taken a cotton to him—even though she had walked away from him.

His thoughts were interrupted by Ma coming over with more people to meet. "Brian, this is Ryan, who owns the general store, and his wife, Mary Elizabeth. You already met Nick."

"Nice meeting you Ryan and Mary Elizabeth. And good to see you again, Nick."

"Hey, Brian, I heard that you wanted to build your own house. That right?"

Brian nodded. "Well, first I thought I'd try to buy one —if there are any available around here."

"There aren't," said Eliza. "I just talked to Mary Elizabeth's father, the president of the bank. All sales go through him, and he said nothing is for sale right now except land." She leaned up and kissed Brian on the cheek. "I'll see you later, Brian. I have to check in the kitchen and see what Granny and Edward are up to. They haven't been out to greet any guests."

"So, yeah, I guess I'll be building my own house, Nick. Why do you ask?"

"Because I have a deal for you! My wife, Rachel, lives in that house across the street from the school. But I'm the deputy and supposed to sleep in the jailhouse at night. Josiah has given me permission to put a second story on the jail, so that Rachel and I and our two boys can live upstairs there. My proposal to you is that I'll help you build your house if you help me build onto the jail!"

"You'd have your family live above the jail? Isn't that dangerous?"

Ryan laughed. "Brian, things have changed since you left—well, more like since Josiah became the sheriff. He keeps a tight hand on the town. There've been some random bad events, but rarely. He's a good sheriff and a good guy. You know, he's married to my sister, Jenna. I think the world of him."

"He seems like a good guy. He offered—well, more like insisted—that my children and I take their house, and they are going to move in here where we're staying now. It's been crowded, but I figured we could manage until I found—or built—a place." Brian turned toward Nick. "So when do we get started?"

"You need to find some land to buy, first."

"I might be able to help with that." Josiah walked up and stood beside the other men. "The land across from my ranch is up for sale. It's quite a few acres, but if you don't want that much, they would probably just sell you what you need. And I can guarantee you'd have great neighbors—us!" Josiah laughed. "Anyway, I can show you the property tomorrow when I bring you over to our place." Josiah hesitated and then looked thoughtful. "Oh. I forgot. How will you get from there to town?"

"He's welcome to my wagon, and we can ask Granny about using Dolly. I only need them on Sunday when I go to, um, town." Ryan shifted on his feet like he was uncomfortable.

"That would be great if Brian could use the wagon. Then he and I can go get some wood for the jailhouse."

"Can you tell me something, please?" Brian looked into each of the men's eyes. "Do you know where my parents are going to get the money for me to buy the land to build a house? I know it's not free. What's all the secrecy about?"

"Well—" began Nick, but Josiah elbowed him.

"Brian, that's not for us—" Josiah started.

Granny walked up to them. "Okay, what's going on with you boys? Can't you talk straight to this fine young man who is now my new grandson?"

Samuel stepped up to them. "Granny, Eliza and I

43

decided that—"

Eliza stepped up beside him. "It's more like *you* decided, Samuel. I never liked keeping secrets from the boy."

Granny stamped her foot. "Oh, tarnation! He's a grown up! What's he going to do? Go blabber it to all the wrong people? Tell him! He has a right to know, so he doesn't think that you robbed a bank to fund him! And tell him how you found him, while you're at it. Tell him *everything*!" Granny put her hands on her hips and looked at Eliza and Samuel. "Go on, tell him now! He deserves to know!"

Samuel looked abashed, but Eliza nodded her head, yes. Josiah shrugged his shoulders and said, "He's your son, Eliza and Samuel. It's your decision."

Brian stood there watching and wondering what was going on. But he liked Granny, and he put his arm around her. "Granny said to tell me, and I think you oughta."

CHAPTER TWELVE

LINDY WANTED TO get out of there. Walking out into the entryway, she searched frantically for Cody, but he was nowhere to be seen. Then she heard Rachel's voice behind her.

"You looking for me?"

"Hi, Rachel. No, I'm looking for Cody. I'm going back to the house now. It's been a long, emotional day."

"Okay, I understand. But why don't you leave Cody here? He's having a blast with Jamie and the other children."

Lindy followed Rachel's eyes and saw the six children running back and forth on the hallway upstairs. "I can't just leave him here and not tell him."

Rachel shrugged. "Why don't you ask him if he wants to stay?"

"Cody! Cody!"

Cody looked through the upstairs railing. He wasn't tall enough to look over it. "Yeah, Mom?"

"Would you like to stay here or go back to the house with me?"

She saw Cody stiffen and his eyes grow wide. "You

don't mean *our* house, right?"

"No, Cody, we're not going back there—ever."

Cody visibly relaxed. "Then I'll stay here." He turned around without another word and raced up and back the hallway with the other children.

"I guess that settles that." Rachel nodded. "Are you sure you don't want to stay? Aren't you having a good time? I could introduce you to more people if you'd like."

Lindy stole a quick glance at Brian who was already surrounded by other people. She sighed and said, "No, I think I need to relax and take it easy for a while. You don't mind, do you?"

"No, no! Make yourself at home! But maybe you should take some more dessert home. I don't think there's anything to eat at the house. You know"—she leaned forward and whispered—"nineteenth century, no refrigeration." She straightened back up. "Well, actually there is. Ryan and Mary Elizabeth have a solar powered refrigerator. And Nick and I have talked about getting one, but just haven't yet. We get by like everybody else *here*."

Lindy nodded. "Okay, Rachel, I'm going to take off now. If Cody gets to be too much, just call me. Oh! I guess you can't! Well, here I go." She hugged Rachel. "Thanks for everything. Bye." And she slipped out the door and walked down the street toward Rachel and Nick's house.

After entering the house, she used the composting toilet that Rachel had showed her earlier. Then she walked straight to her bedroom and flopped on the bed, clothes and all. "Her bedroom" was Jamie and Oscar's old room. The two boys now had to sleep in the living

46

room, while Lindy and Cody slept in their bed. The kids said they didn't mind, though. Oscar said that he had never had a bed until he was adopted by Nick and Rachel. Poor kid must have had a hard time of it. And Jamie said that he was happy to have his friend Cody staying at his house.

That thought made Lindy think that her life wasn't so bad after all. She didn't think that she should look at it as a former abuse victim—she felt her lip and decided that perhaps "former" wasn't quite right—but she should look at how generous life was that she could come to this wonderful place and be safe. So what if there were no cell phones, no refrigeration, and only composting toilets. None of that really mattered, though, did it? What mattered is that they were safe here. After all, the sheriff wore a gun.

Then her thoughts drifted to Brian, which made her smile. When he took her hands in his, all she could remember was how warm his hands had been. She had backed up and been taken off guard, yes, but she didn't know then that he had been widowed. He had no wife. Nothing for her to be uptight about. He was single. *And* he was incredibly handsome. He looked like his father, Samuel, only younger. Green eyes, light brown hair, and muscular. Thinking about him made her heart beat faster, but she didn't want it to. She had just been punched in the mouth by a man! Did she really want to fall for another one so quickly?

But Brian was different from Ray. There was nothing similar about the two men at all. Lindy had seen how Brian was with his children—he couldn't have been any more loving and patient. She liked that in a man. And if she was going to fall for a man here in the nineteenth

47

(Resetting)

century, she thought that Brian was perfect for that. Handsome, kind, and available. Her breath caught in her chest, though. After what happened with Ray, could she ever open herself to a man and allow herself to be vulnerable again? The warmth of Brian's hands came to mind, and she thought, yes, with him she could open herself. With him she could be vulnerable. And why did she feel that way? Because Brian felt safe to her. Brian could comfort her and protect her—from men like Ray.

CHAPTER THIRTEEN

GRANNY LOOKED RIGHT at Samuel. "This is ridiculous! If you don't tell him, I will!"

Without answering, Samuel stomped away. Eliza looked at Granny. "If you want to, go ahead. You've already started it."

Granny looked up at Brian, who towered above her. "Let's all go to the back of the kitchen, first, so nobody overhears us."

Eliza, Ryan, Josiah, Nick, and Brian followed Granny into the kitchen. Then Granny began. "Brian, me, and several other people in this town, all come from *the future.*"

Brian burst out laughing. "That's all you can up with? Oh, come on. Granny you were right. This is ridiculous. Now tell me the truth." Then Brian noticed that he was the only one laughing. They all looked at him with serious expressions on their faces. He looked from one face to the other. "You're all hornswoggling me—aren't you?"

Josiah grabbed Brian's arm and pulled him out of the kitchen back into the restaurant. "Have you had any of these desserts yet? I bet you've never tasted anything like them before in your whole life. I never had, and I'm from Boston!"

"Oh, come on," said Brian, backing away from the sweets.

Josiah scooped up some Neopolitan ice cream and put it on a plate. Beside it, he put some Rocky Road ice cream. "Here. Eat it." Then he leaned forward and whispered, "They don't have these in the nineteenth century yet. Ryan brought them back from *there*."

Brian took a spoon and put some Rocky Road into his mouth. "It's delicious, but eating it won't convince me."

"The Neopolitan! Eat the Neopolitan!" Josiah pointed to the ice cream on Brian's plate.

Brian put some ice cream into his mouth and closed his eyes with satisfaction. "Yes, it's delicious, but no, I still don't believe. Bella had an ice cream maker and she was always putting strange ingredients together. Never anything this uniform"—he pointed to the Neopolitan —"but it could be done."

"Oh, tarnation, grandson! We're telling you the truth here! What do we have to do? Take you—"

"Wait!" said Ryan. "I know how to convince him! I'll be right back. Where's Sarah?" After searching unsuccessfully for Sarah in the room they were in, Ryan rushed off toward the entryway.

"What's he want with Sarah? We've got a man here to convince of the truth!" Granny said.

Nick leaned over to whisper in Granny's ear. "Sarah still has her cell phone. She carries it everywhere."

"No way!" said Granny and cackled with laughter. "She can't use it here! Why would she do that?"

Nick shrugged. "She can't seem to do without it. Look, here they come."

Sarah was headed their way, with Ryan following several paces behind smiling. Walking right up to Brian, she held out her hand and said, "Hi! I'm Sarah! I'm married to Matthew, the saloonkeeper."

"Nice meeting you, Sarah," said Brian, wondering what they were going to come up with next.

"I'm supposed to give this to you to convince you of something." Sarah fished something out of her pocket and handed it to him.

Brian turned it over in his hand. "I don't recognize what it's made of, but so what?"

"Sarah, turn it on for him!" said Josiah.

"Oh, yeah. Here, Brian." She touched a small button on the phone, and it lit up.

It was not what he expected at all, and he might have dropped the object except that everyone thought it was very valuable. "What do you do with it?" There were tiny pictures on the front of it, but Brian didn't know what they meant or if they meant anything. Were they a new kind of writing from the future?

"Here, let me show you." She touched the top of the object twice and pictures started moving across the screen. When he looked more carefully, it was Sarah riding a horse that was jumping over a couple of logs. But in a minute, the pictures had stopped moving.

"Do it again!" said Brian.

"Here, touch it right there, and it will repeat," she said.

He touched it with his finger, and the moving pictures began again, the same as before. When it finished, he touched it again. And then he did it a third time. Brian nodded his head and handed the phone back to Sarah. "All right. This doesn't belong in this century. Tell me

51

more." He looked around at the people. "Ma, why did you whisper thank you to Jenna, and why did Jenna say that she found me?"

Eliza moved her head up and down. "Yes, well, I don't understand it, but—"

"I'll tell him, Eliza," said Nick. "Brian, there is a new invention called a computer—Sarah's phone is actually a small one. But on the computer, there is something called the Internet where you can look stuff up like, like an encyclopedia!"

"When Jenna fell in love with me, she wanted to make sure that I wasn't going to die in a gunfight and leave her a widow, so she looked up my death on the Internet." Josiah chimed in. "She discovered that I'm not going to die for a good long time. But then she got the idea to look *you* up, because Eliza had told her that you and your brother had died in the Civil War, but she had a feeling you were alive."

"You did, Ma?" Brian asked.

Eliza nodded, and Josiah continued. "Jenna discovered that you had died in Red Bluff and not in Virginia. It took her awhile to tell Eliza, though."

"Yes, I wondered why she waited," said Eliza.

Josiah shrugged. "For starters, it's not an easy thing to tell someone. And what if she was wrong? But I think Jenna was really uncomfortable about it."

"Then it was a matter of going to the battle where you were supposed to have died. We stopped by many places before we found the right one," said Eliza.

"All right. That explains how you found me, but how about the money? I don't understand what the future has to do with me not needing money."

Josiah reached into his pocket and pulled out some

change. He held up a penny. "How much is this worth?"

Brian laughed. "Now you're joking with me. It's worth a penny!"

"Yes, it's worth a penny here, but in the future, it could be worth fifteen or twenty dollars. How about this?" Josiah held up a ten-cent piece.

"It's worth ten cents."

"*Here* it's worth ten cents." Josiah glanced at the date. "I don't know offhand, but *there* it could be worth twenty-five dollars or two hundred or more." He reached into his pocket and pulled out a gold dollar and held it up for Brian. "These are generally worth three hundred dollars, but sometimes much more."

"Zack—you'll meet Zack sometime, he lives in the future, but he's from here—he found a coin worth more than a million dollars!" said Nick.

"This is unbelievable," said Brian, shaking his head.

"And while your Ma and Pa were gone, and Edward and I were running the place, we collected lots of coins worth a bunch of money. We've been finding some really good ones, since the stagecoach started coming to town. I think you're set for life!" Granny put her hands on her hips and nodded decisively.

Brian took another bite of pie and ice cream and looked at each of the faces around him. "All right then. When can I go *there* to see for myself?"

CHAPTER FOURTEEN

LINDY WAS SLEEPING when Nick and Rachel came home from the party with the three boys, but the commotion woke her. Cody came in tiptoeing, got himself undressed and into his pajamas, and then slid in beside her. He whispered in her ear, "I love you, Mommy," and then he turned over and a few minutes later, she could tell he was sleeping. Since he had made such an effort to be quiet, she didn't want to spoil it for him by being awake.

When Lindy woke the next morning, she had that moment of disorientation when you awake in a strange place, but she figured it out right away. Her lip and her jaw hurt, and her legs still felt sore. She tentatively reached up to see if he had loosened any of her teeth, but they were all okay. Her stay at the hospital when he broke her ribs, had also included losing a molar from where he had hit her on the side of the face. How did she live like that for so long? He was always hitting her, shoving her, slapping her and slapping Cody, and she had put up with it for *years*. Because afterward, he would always apologize, bring her flowers, and treat her wonderfully for a day or two until something ticked him off.

Then the cycle would start all over again. But she thought he loved her. And she thought that someday he might even get over it and everything would return to "normal." The truth was, there never was any normal. Even before he began hitting her, he would constantly insult her and put her down.

Lindy sighed and looked over at Cody, still sleeping peacefully on the pillow next to her. That little man deserved a father he could depend on, not one that he was afraid of. Her mind sped back to the previous night when Brian said that they should get married. Would Brian be that kind of man? Oh, yeah. Remembering how he had been with his children, she had no doubts of that.

Why had she run off like that last night, she asked herself. Because she had almost told him about the future when she realized she shouldn't. Emotionally, it was overwhelming. When she thought about it, she realized that she probably shouldn't have gone to that party last night at all. Too much had happened in the day that she had to process. But if she hadn't gone last night, then she probably would have kept Cody home with her, and it was good for him to get out like that and play with the other kids. She could tell he had a great time, and she knew that was good for him. It had been an emotional day for him, too.

Thinking back on Brian and his warm hands, and how he had looked at her, she wondered when she would see him again. She knew one thing: she hoped it was soon. He made her feel like a woman—and she had not felt like a woman for a long, long time. With Ray, she had felt like a punching bag for far too long. It had been so long since she had opened up with a man enough to even give her a chance to feel like a woman. But with Brian, it felt automatic, she was comfortable with him right away. She laughed about how they had finished each other's sentences.

Cody stirred, and she kissed him on the cheek. He opened his eyes and looked around. "Where are we, Mommy?"

"Remember, we're staying at your friend Jamie's house. You had fun with him and the other kids last night. Remember?"

A smile played across his lips. "Yeah, I had fun. I wasn't scared."

His comment silenced her, and she drew in a sharp breath. She felt guilty that she hadn't taken him away from that environment before. And she chastised herself that she should have known that Ray would come back to the house like he did. Cody had been doing so well, and now he might even have a relapse of what he was like after Ray sent her to the hospital. But being here and seeing him here—he seemed to be handling everything really well.

Cody interrupted her thoughts. "Mommy, thank you for bringing me here. I feel safe here. I don't think Daddy can find us here, do you?"

"I sure hope not, Cody."

"Well, even if he does, Sheriff Josiah wears a gun. He'll protect us."

"Rise and shine, everybody! It's almost time for breakfast!" Rachel, rattling plates, called out from the kitchen.

"We'll be there in a minute!" Lindy pulled her feet out from under the covers and sat on the edge of the bed. "Come on, Cody, let's get ready." While Lindy dressed, Cody dressed himself. And then they took turns using the composting toilet at the back of the house. Rachel had told her that a few of the "newcomers" had them, but the locals hadn't caught on yet and still used outhouses, which everyone called "the necessary."

When Lindy got to the table, the boys were almost finished eating. Cody kissed her on the cheek, and then followed the boys into the living room to play with a wooden train. Lindy sank into the chair beside Rachel. "What a day yesterday was, huh?" She reached up and felt her lip. "It was tough, and I have the scars to prove it!" She and Rachel laughed, and Rachel poured her a cup of coffee. "All the conveniences of home, huh, Rachel?"

"Not quite, but this is definitely home. I'd *never* return to the twenty-first century—at least not for any longer than a trip to a good restaurant!" Rachel took a sip of her coffee and put it down on the table. "Nick feels the same way. This is home for us now, and always will be."

"Where is Nick?"

"He works today—Josiah has weekends off. So Nick's at the office."

That struck Lindy funny. Rachel said he was at the *office*, like he was wearing a suit and working in downtown twenty-first-century Red Bluff, when instead, he was wearing a gun and sitting in a nineteenth-century sheriff's office. That train of thought made her realize that she needed to work. "I was thinking, Rachel. I need to find a job, so I can support myself and Cody."

"No, you don't. All we do is go to the bank, spend some time looking at their coins, check the list that Zack gave us, and pull out the valuable ones. Then someone takes them to Zack, he cashes them in for more of *our* money, and we're set. So, you don't need a job—you just need to spend some time at the bank. I'll give you Zack's list."

"Yeah, but Rachel, what will I do all day? The boredom will drive me crazy." She looked up suddenly and said, "Oh, no! I never quit my job! They're probably wondering where I am! And I didn't even have a chance to call my mother. I'm going to have to go back."

"Is that safe? How about somebody else makes those calls for you?"

Rachel nodded. "Yes, you're right. That would be better. I don't want to go back. But anyway, what do you think about a job? I can't just sit around all day."

"You know, maybe the hotel could use some help. Last night when I talked to Granny, she had said that she and Edward want to retire permanently, so Eliza and Samuel might need some help. Mary Elizabeth has been helping out occasionally, but less and less because the store had gotten busy, and Ryan needs her there. You would be a perfect fit!"

Lindy raised her eyebrows and nodded, a slight smile on her face. "Yeah, a perfect fit."

Rachel noticed. "What's *that* about?"

"I met Brian last night. He's very handsome, and he's not married. I think I could really like him. When we finished each other's sentences, he said that we should get married—he was kidding, of course, but I wouldn't mind seeing more of him. You know?"

"Ooh la la," said Rachel.

CHAPTER FIFTEEN

WHEN BRIAN OPENED his eyes, fresh from sleep, his first thought was that he was in yet another hotel room. Then he remembered. He was home. The boys were still sleeping, but Amy was sitting up in her bed playing with her doll. She had already used the strange necessary that Josiah had explained was something from the twenty-first century—but an Old West version of it, so no one would take notice. That made him think about the previous night.

Two wondrous things had happened last night: he had met Lindy, whom he thought of as the most beautiful girl in the world, and he had finally found out what all the secrecy during the whole trip was about. Several people in town had come here from the future! It was difficult to believe, but the object that Sarah had was surely not from this time. And there was something a little *different* about the people who came from *there*: Ryan, Jenna, Kat, and Granny, all related; Nick and Rachel, married, they both came from there; Sarah; and Lindy was from there, too. And then there was Zack, born here, but now living in the twenty-first century. He'd probably meet Zack when they traveled to the future. But out of all those people, the only one who mattered to him at that moment was Lindy.

Ah, Lindy. He exhaled slowly, smiled, and wondered when he'd see her again. He hoped it would be soon. But today, he and the children would move to Jenna and Josiah's ranch. How generous of them to give up their home and move in here. Of course there were only the two of them and the infant, it would be easier for them in this space. Still, it was inconvenient for them. And Brian was very grateful for their offer.

Oh! Josiah could be here anytime to pick him up. He swung his legs over the bed and said, "Come on, boys, time to get up! We're moving today!" Then he looked over at Amy, quietly playing with her doll. "Morning, sweetheart. Did you sleep well?"

"Yes, Papa." She climbed off the bed, walked over to him, and put her arms around his neck. "I love you, Papa."

"I love you, too, sweetie. We need to get ready now. Can you get yourself dressed?"

Amy nodded and started going through the bag that carried her clothes. Brian got dressed quickly, after pulling the covers off the boys to encourage them. They rubbed their eyes sleepily, but got dressed without much delay. Then the four of them walked out into the entryway.

"'Bout time you got up, grandson," said Granny. "We've been up for hours already! It must be nice to lounge around until noon."

Brian, taken aback, glanced out the front window and saw that the sun was barely up. He shook his head and smiled at Granny, as the kids surrounded her begging for hugs and kisses.

Edward, his grandfather, stepped out of the kitchen and smiled when he saw him. He walked over and put his hand on Brian's shoulder. "Brian, I can't tell you how good it is to see you again. For so many years, we thought, we thought—" Brian noticed tears in his eyes, so he looked away.

"Stop your blubbering, old man, and let's get these children some breakfast. They're moving to a new house today, and it's a dang fine house, even if I do have to say so myself. Oh! I just did!"

"Old woman, if you don't behave, I'm going to have to beat you in front of these children. Is that what you want?"

That shocked Brian until Granny cackled with laughter and took Edward's hand. Together they walked into the restaurant kitchen, swinging their linked hands. He liked how they were together, easy, laughing, affectionate. Once, he had that with Bella. And he hoped to have that again sometime soon—with Lindy.

Brian and the boys sat down at a table, and a few minutes later, Granny and Grampy came out laden down with plates. There were eggs, bacon, fried potatoes, and toast and butter. It looked delicious.

When Brian was almost finished eating—the food was so good that he didn't want to stop until his plate was empty—Josiah walked in with a dog. After putting his fork down, Brian chewed up the last of his meal, stood up, and put out his hand. "Josiah. Good to see you. Who's this?" Brian put his hand out for the dog to sniff it. "Hi, fella."

"Ah, my dog, Bingo. Jenna's dog, Jet, is still in the wagon." When Brian started to stand up, Josiah said,

"You don't have to rush. I still have to unload our stuff from the wagon."

"No, I'm fine. Let me help you."

As Brian approached the wagon, he saw that Jenna was still sitting in the front, feeding the baby. Brian averted his eyes and said, "Morning, Jenna."

"Oh, hi, Brian. I told Josiah to tell you, but in case he forgets, I'll tell you now. I changed all the sheets for your family. Everything is clean and fresh."

"Thanks, Jenna. I appreciate you both going to all this inconvenience for me."

"No trouble at all, Brian. We're glad you're home. And safe."

Brian nodded. "Me, too. It's good to be back—and especially good to see Ma and Pa and Grampy."

"Grampy? Oh, we're going to have to tease Edward about that, Josiah!"

"You can, Jenna. I won't have any part of your teasing!" From the wagon, Josiah pulled out a strange bag with straps on it and handed it to Brian. "Yes, this is from there, Brian. You'll be seeing a lot of these. And you should get one. They're called *backpacks*, and they're very convenient, especially if you're on horseback. Do you ride?"

"Yes, but I don't have a horse."

"We'll have to let Ezra at the livery know what you're looking for. He has an uncanny ability to find the exact horse that you want."

"I'd like to get some horses for the children, too. Can he find another little one like I saw over there? It would be the perfect size for Amy."

"Ah, that one is from *there*. We can find you one of those, too. No worries."

After they had toted all Josiah's and Jenna's bags inside and all of Brian's bags outside, they were ready to go. Eliza and Samuel came out of their living area and hugged Brian. "It's so good to have you home, son," said Pa. Ma just hugged him and couldn't say anything because of the tears running down her face.

"It's good to be home."

Willie ran up to him. "Pa, can I go with you, please? I can help with the bags!"

Brian laughed. "You didn't help with these!"

"I was still eating. Please? I want to see our new house."

Brian put a hand on his shoulder. "Willie, we'll all go over there later. Right now, Josiah and I are going. All right?"

"All right," he said and with head hanging low, walked back into the restaurant.

"Okay, shall we get going?" asked Josiah.

"Yes, I'm ready. Let's go." Brian stuck his head in the restaurant and called out, "Bye, children. I'll see you in a few hours. Please behave for your Grammy and Grampy."

"We will, Pa," sang out a trio of voices.

"Bye," Brian said, as he hugged Ma and Pa before stepping out the door. "Thank you so much for coming to get me. It's good to be home."

CHAPTER SIXTEEN

LINDY AND RACHEL walked up the street with Jamie and Cody following close behind. Oscar, the older boy, had walked up to the sheriff's office to be with Nick. According to Rachel, he had been a real pistol before—the worst behaved kid in her class—until they adopted him. Once he was shown a little love and consideration, he settled right down. Now, he wanted to spend every spare minute with Nick, whom he called *Pa*.

When Rachel opened the door of the hotel for her, Lindy felt nervous. It felt like a job interview—well, it was—in the nineteenth century. Eliza and Granny were behind the front desk. They both looked up when Lindy entered. The two boys ran into the restaurant when they heard the other kids playing.

Rachel walked up first. "Lindy, this is Eliza and Granny. Eliza and Granny, this is Lindy, from *there*. She was wondering if you had any work available."

"She's hired!" Granny pounded her fist on the desk for emphasis. "Edward and I have had enough of this working life, and we want to retire!"

"Hallo, Lindy," said Eliza. "I would need you to work

the front desk on occasion and work in the restaurant. Would that be something that you'd be interested in?"

"Yes, definitely!" Lindy felt excited that it was working out.

"What happened here?" Granny pointed to her own lip. "It looks like someone punched you in the mouth."

Lindy sighed, nodded, and looked down. "Yes, my ex-husband always was good at hitting what he aimed at."

"Ah," said Eliza, "that's what brings you to town, then, huh?"

"Exactly. I had to find a place where he couldn't find me. This was it. He just got out of prison—for putting me in the hospital—and I thought he'd leave us alone, but unfortunately, he didn't." She touched her own lip and pulled her finger away when it hurt. "I hope this goes away soon, I'm self-conscious about it."

"Oh, you don't have to be self-conscious," said Granny. "The whole town will know about it in a day or two, anyway!" She laughed and shrugged her shoulders. "Small town living, you know? Everybody knows everybody's business. It's the charm of the place *and* the draw-back."

Eliza looked at Granny. "I see that you haven't lost any of your sense of humor, Granny!"

Lindy, uncomfortable, looked away. Rachel put her arm around her in a hug. "Lindy! You have nothing to be ashamed about! *He* hit you!"

"Yeah, but I stayed with him way too long."

"Are you still married to the creep?" asked Granny.

"No, I divorced him last year after he put me in the hospital."

Granny came out from behind the desk and looked into Lindy's eyes. "Listen. Some people need more opportunities to learn the lesson. It's nothing to be ashamed of! You finally learned? Right? You're not with him anymore? No, you're not. Lesson learned! Now chalk it up to experience! Bad experience, yes," she chuckled, "but experience nonetheless. Let your lip heal and forget about the heel!" She beamed at everyone. "See what I just did! Heal and heel? Get it?"

Everyone laughed. Eliza came out from behind the desk. "Lindy, can you start tomorrow?"

"Yeah! Sure! That would be great!"

Granny squinted her eyes at Lindy. "Hey. Aren't you the girl that my new grandson was flirting with yesterday at the party?"

Lindy smiled shyly and nodded. And she felt herself blush.

"So, it looked pretty obvious that he liked you. Do you like him as well?" Granny raised her eyebrows.

"I think he's very handsome and kind. And I like kind."

"Eliza! Eliza!" Granny called out as if Eliza was in the next room instead of right next to her. "We have a supper to arrange!"

At that moment, Cody and Jamie ran out of the restaurant followed by Amy chasing them. Lindy watched and didn't say anything.

"All right, Lindy. So tonight, you are invited to supper right in there." Eliza pointed to her living quarters through the door by the front desk. Brian will be there."

Cody ran up to Lindy and grabbed her hand. Lindy leaned down and kissed him on the top of his head, and then he ran back off.

"And your son is invited, too," said Eliza. "Rachel, you, Nick, and the boys are welcome, too."

"No, I think we should stay home, so you can have a nice, little intimate dinner for *ten*!"

Eliza nodded and laughed. Granny cackled, and Lindy didn't understand what was funny. But she would see Brian at dinner tonight, and that's all that mattered. And the people here were already making her feel like this was her home. Which was good—because it was.

CHAPTER SEVENTEEN

BRIAN EASILY BOOSTED himself up into the wagon to sit next to Josiah. The dog, Bingo, sat in the back of the wagon. He felt like this was the first day of the rest of his life. It would feel better when he and the children were living in their *own* house, but he felt like that wasn't too far off. Josiah shook the reins and said, "Come on, Dolly." And they were off.

"So Dolly is Granny's horse? She's pretty."

"When Granny rides, which is seldom, she rides Dolly. Although Dolly is Jenna's horse—well, our horse. But we always ask Granny before we use her. And Ryan has a standing agreement with Granny that he can use Dolly every Sunday unless Granny notifies him beforehand." Josiah clucked to Dolly to get her to go faster.

"Where does Ryan go every Sunday?" Brian asked.

Josiah looked at him. "He goes *there*—picks up items for the store, gets items that the *new* people have requested, and just lately, he's begun changing money."

"Changing money? What do you mean?"

"You know how we explained how valuable some of the coins are from the nineteenth century? He takes the valuable ones and trades them in for more of the ones that aren't so valuable. That way, the people from here don't have to make the trip *there* so often."

"Oh! Is it a long way?"

Josiah laughed. "It takes less than an hour on horse-back. Some of us go back almost every week—to go to dinner or buy items that aren't available here. But others rarely go back. Jenna and I used to go every week before Milo was born, now we don't go as often. But Rachel and Nick haven't gone back for ages. When they first adopted the boys, they went back there to get them some clothes. But since then, not so much. So Ryan exchanges money for them."

"It all sounds so complex. I'd love to go, though." Brian looked ahead nodding his head and thinking. "Traveling made me confuse all the days, but isn't to-morrow Sunday?"

"Yes, it is. And I suppose you would like to go along when Ryan goes to town?"

"You bet I would!"

"You're already on the list! You and Nick will go get some lumber for the jailhouse while Ryan does his food shopping."

Brian nodded. "I can hardly wait." He smiled to him-self and imagined what it would be like *there*. "Josiah, do you know why my parents didn't want to tell me about all that?"

"I'm close to your folks, Brian. And it's my opinion that it was your Pa, not your Ma, who was against it."

"Yeah, that sounds right, Josiah. There were a couple times that Ma almost told me. But why would he be so against it?"

"He's never been there."

69

"Never? Really? He wasn't curious?"

"He says he has no desire to go. Eliza went after Jenna told her—that was a year ago, and she's never gone back. I don't think Samuel wants her to."

"Granny's from *there*, too, right? Has Grampy ever gone?"

"Edward went once. He didn't want to, but Granny had to have a medical procedure done that hasn't been invented here yet. It couldn't be helped. She was supposed to come back the same day, but when Edward found out that she had to stay overnight, he went right over there. I don't think he did anything but go straight to the hospital, and then they returned the following day. He's never gone back. And Granny has no desire to go back, either, so it works out for them." Josiah pointed to their left. "Hey, we're almost there. Look up here on the left."

Brian looked as Dolly turned into a small ranch on their left. It was the ranch he had already seen. "I saw this from the stagecoach. I thought it looked so nice that I wanted one like it—only bigger!"

"Yeah, with three kids, you'll need bigger, that's for sure. But I think you'll be more comfortable here than at the hotel." Dolly stopped in front of the house, Josiah and Brian stepped down and grabbed some bags to tote inside. Josiah opened the door and led the way inside. "Here's the bigger bedroom—it's the one with the composting toilet."

"Oh! You have one, too?"

Josiah smiled. "We were the first to have one! Although I have to admit that it was Jenna's sister Kat's idea." They put the bags on the bed, and Josiah led the way to the other bedroom. "Here's the smaller room, but they both have double beds. And see here"—Josiah walked to the couch—"Jenna put a sleeping bag on the couch."

Brian opened the top flap to see what it was. "Oh, that's some pumpkins! I've never seen anything like it. That will be great!"

"Let's finish carrying everything inside, and then I'll show you the property across the road that's for sale."

They finished a few minutes later and jumped into the wagon. Then Josiah guided Dolly across the road. They moved forward until they got to some thick trees, and Josiah stopped the wagon and got out. "See, plenty of trees to build a home with, but also plenty of pasture."

"Josiah, it looks great. I'd like to raise some cattle, and this would be perfect. I want it!"

When they rode home, Brian could barely contain his excitement. "My own place! I can't believe I'm going to have my own place! And Nick is going to help me build it! Everything is working out perfectly!"

"Now all you need is a wife!" said Josiah.

Brian sat in the wagon nodding, with the fingers of one hand on his mouth. "Yeah, I sure do."

"Well, I'm not going to say there's plenty of women in town, but—"

"I only need one." He turned toward Josiah. "Do you know Lindy?"

"I know *of* her."

"Do you know how she got that?" Brian pointed to his mouth. "She's beautiful, but I couldn't help noticing that. I didn't feel right asking her, but I'd like to know."

"Yeah, her husband—"

"Oh, no! She's married?"

"Not so fast, big guy. Let me finish. Her *ex*-husband, I

should have said. He just got out of prison, and he came back to the house, hit her, and threatened her. That's why she came here."

"Is she going to stay here?"

"As far as I know. She doesn't feel safe over *there*, anymore. But you'll have to ask her about that." Josiah looked at Brian. "So you're sweet on her, huh?"

Brian smiled shyly. "I think she's beautiful. We talked some at the party, and we were already finishing each other's sentences! I told her we should get married!"

"Sounds like you're moving too fast, Brian."

"Yeah, I think I might have scared her off. But I also think that she likes me, too, so I'm hoping I can fix it."

"Well, if your mother gets wind of this, she'll invite you both over to supper to seal the deal! How do you think Jenna and I got together?" Josiah laughed.

Brian nodded, smiled, and hoped that Josiah was right. He couldn't wait to see Lindy again.

CHAPTER EIGHTEEN

RACHEL HAD GOTTEN Lindy all dressed up in a beautiful long skirt and white ruffled blouse. She also said that she'd tell Nick to pick her up some long dresses when he went with Ryan the following day. Lindy would be glad to get some of her own clothes to wear. If she had known in advance that they didn't wear jeans here, she could have brought some with her. When, she thought? When would she have done that? There was no time. She had to get away from Ray, and she had to do that quickly. Borrowing would have to do for now, and she hoped that soon she'd have her own clothes.

As she and Cody walked up the street, holding hands, Cody seemed awfully enthusiastic about just having dinner—or supper, as they called it here. Maybe he was mirroring what she felt. Lindy was so excited to see Brian again that she could barely contain herself. Unconsciously, she quickened her pace and Cody had to skip to keep up. "Slow down, Mommy!" he said.

Lindy chuckled. "Oh, sorry, Cody. I guess I'm excited to get there."

"Me, too, but we don't have to run. It's just a few more

steps."

"You're right, Cody." She slowed her pace, reached the hotel in a few more steps like Cody said, and opened the door.

Eliza stood by the front desk when they entered. As soon as Eliza saw them, she said, "Come in, come in. Everyone is already sitting down." Holding out her arm showing the way, Eliza welcomed them with a big grin.

"Oh, I hope we aren't late!"

"No, no. We're all early!" said Eliza, following her inside.

When Lindy looked up at the people seated at the table, she realized what Rachel had meant when she had said an intimate dinner for ten. Samuel sat at the far end of the table, and the other end was vacant for, she assumed, Eliza. On the side of the table closest to the window, sat Brian at the close end with his older son next to him, and Granny and Edward in the two seats closest to Samuel. On the near side of the table, sat the younger son and the little girl, Amy. The two seats closest to Eliza were empty, and one of them was right across from Brian. As she looked up from assessing the situation, she found him watching her with an appreciative look on his face.

Cody started to sit in the end seat, but Eliza moved him over and said, "You sit in the middle here next to Amy, all right?"

"Yes," said Cody shyly.

"And you sit right here, my dear." Eliza pulled out the chair across from Brian for Lindy and then sat down at the end of table. "Tonight, we will be treated like royalty." She she picked up a bell that was sitting on the table, and she rang it.

Josiah backed out of the kitchen door, wearing a white apron, and carrying a plate of food in both hands. His dog, Bingo, followed him. "Tonight, I will be serving foods from both *there* and here. First on the menu is the delicious entree called spaghetti pie. And next is succotash." He put the plates on the table and added, "And I'd like you to know that I did not spend the whole day in the kitchen slaving away to create these fine delicacies. You can thank Eliza and Granny for that. I am merely your humble servant!"

He crossed one arm behind him and one arm in front of him and bowed from the waist, making everyone laugh. Then he leaned over, squeezed Brian's shoulder, winked, and whispered loud enough for everyone to hear, "I told you!" After that, he nodded to Lindy and returned to the kitchen, re-emerging a moment later with a large bowl of peas. "And imported straight from"—he glanced at Samuel who was scowling—"*there*, we have fresh green peas." Josiah made a big show of bowing again, and then returned to the kitchen.

"Go ahead, dear," Eliza said to Lindy, "take what you'd like. You and Brian are the guests of honor tonight."

"What about us?" asked Archie indignantly.

"Yes, of course, you, too," said Samuel. When Cody squirmed in his seat, Samuel added, "You, too, Cody, of course!"

Lindy used a pie server to cut the spaghetti pie and put the piece on her plate. It had a spaghetti noodle crust with hamburger, tomatoes, and olives inside, and cheese on top. It looked delicious. Then she used the serving spoon to take some succotash. She had never had it before, but it looked like corn and beans mixed together.

And then she took some peas. When she raised her eyes after serving herself, she saw that Brian was watching her every move. She smiled at him and started eating. His gaze was so intense that although she wasn't looking at him, she could feel his eyes on her. In all the time that she and Ray were together, he had never looked at her like that. That was probably part of the problem.

At first, the conversation was just general about what had been going on since Eliza and Samuel left, especially about the stage coming to town, which meant the hotel had gotten busier. The conversation progressed to the two marriages that had happened since they left: Ryan and Mary Elizabeth, and Nick and Rachel. Then Granny looked at Lindy and asked, "Lindy, what did you do for work over *there*?"

Before Lindy had a chance to answer, Archie said, "Pa, Willie threw a pea at me!"

Brian, his eyes never off Lindy except for the seconds it took to get his food on his fork, said without thinking, "Give it back to him."

"What?" asked Archie. "Give it back to him?" Brian nodded without looking at his son. "All right," said Archie, drawing out the words. "Here's your pea back and another one for bothering me."

The peas hit Willie in the face, and he looked up, astounded. "And these are for you!" He picked the two peas up and two more and threw them at Archie. One of the peas hit Amy by mistake, so she reached into the serving plate of peas, took out a handful, and threw them at Willie. A full food fight followed. Granny cackled with laughter, Samuel cleared his throat loudly, and when Brian realized what was happening, he jumped up from his chair, knocking it over backwards, and shouted at the children while pointing out the door, "Go to your rooms, now!"

"Grandson," said Granny innocently, "they don't have rooms here. Remember?"

Brian scowled at Granny, threw his napkin on the table, and followed the children through the door. Eliza, Samuel, Granny, and Edward were on their hands and knees on the floor picking up the peas. Lindy scooted out of her chair, but when she started kneeling, she felt Brian's strong—and warm—hands gently on her helping her up.

"Oh, no," said Brian. "This is damage from my children. Not yours. Cody sat there the whole time like a perfect angel. You and Cody just sit there and eat. I'll handle this. Ma, Pa, Granny, Grampy, you all eat, too. This is my responsibility." Everyone stood up from picking up peas and sat back down at the table. Brian was on his knees picking up peas while the rest of them finished supper.

Lindy started to protest, but Granny had glanced at her, surreptitiously shaking her head no and with her finger over her mouth in a "shhh" gesture. So Lindy continued eating. Cody had stopped eating and pressed against her so tightly that she thought he might push her off the chair. She knew why he hadn't participated in the food fight. He had witnessed so much violent throwing by his father, that it scared him. Lindy found that out when he had refused to play dodge ball at school, and she had asked Cody's psychologist about it. More issues caused by Ray. Would they ever go away, she wondered.

CHAPTER NINETEEN

BRIAN WAS IN a fine pucker—on his hands and knees picking up peas and squished peas from when the children left the room. When he finished with the peas that were on the floor, he followed the trail of more squished peas all the way into the restaurant where he had left the children. The three of them sat there, silent, with their arms tensely crossed over their chests.

Brian didn't say a word and returned to the dining room table, sat down, and began eating again. But he didn't look up at Lindy anymore. He wasn't mad at her, but he was completely embarrassed at what his children had done. Never in their young lives had they ever done anything like that. He sighed and put another bite of succotash in his mouth. Then again, they had been through a lot. Brian knew that leaving the farm in Virginia was a huge step for them, because they had left behind the only reminder of their mother that they had —the grave at the edge of the farm that he knew they all visited every day. Shaking his head, he sighed again, but still didn't look up. His poor children.

Eliza interrupted his thoughts. "Well, well, this didn't

exactly go as planned. Lindy, how about tomorrow night? Are you busy? Can Rachel watch Cody for you? We'll try this again *without* the children."

Brian didn't want to look up. If she never wanted to have anything to do with him ever again, he couldn't blame her. And he didn't want to see her face when she said no. It felt like she was going to say no, until he felt something move under the table. Then she sat up straighter at the same time that he caught Granny's movement out of the corner of his eye. She pointed at Lindy with a grim expression. When he heard Lindy clear her throat to speak, he took a chance and looked up.

He wasn't sure if she saw him or not, but she said, "All right. I guess so." Then she stood up, pulling Cody up with her, thanked Eliza for supper, said "Good-bye, everyone" without addressing anyone—including him—directly, and she marched out the door with Cody in tow.

At that moment, Josiah once again backed out of the kitchen holding two plates: one with a chocolate cake, and the other with two halves of two different pies, both from the previous night, probably. "And here's des— Where did everybody go?"

Brian stood up abruptly, his chair falling behind him. He picked it up, mumbled, "Thanks for supper, Ma," and stomped out the door. It was just as well, he thought, as he pushed open the front door to the hotel and walked through. Falling in love was not what he needed to do right now. Building a house was what he needed to do. Get his life together. Go *there*. He didn't have time for a woman right now—at least not an ordinary woman.

His shoulders slumped, and he exhaled slowly. Lindy was no ordinary woman. Brian shuffled down the street snorting and sighing at intervals. Well, he may not be ready for a woman, but he definitely wanted *her*. There was no talking himself out of it. Although he wasn't sure if he was really *falling in love* with her, it was undoubtedly more than a passing interest. He liked the way she moved, the way she talked; he liked the way she was with Cody.

Brian walked into the livery searching to see where Ezra had put Dolly and the wagon. "You lookin' for the wagon, Brian?" called a voice from the back.

"Yup."

"I'll hook her up for ya. Just wait there."

A minute later, Ezra stopped Dolly right in front of him and climbed out of the wagon. "Here ya go."

"Thanks so much, Ezra. I appreciate it." Brian jumped into the wagon and asked Dolly to move forward. Dolly walked straight forward, and as they went past the house on the corner, Brian looked into the window. There was Lindy, tucking Cody into bed, and kissing him good night. Hesitating for a moment so he could watch her, but not long enough for her to see him, he decided that his life could wait. Building the house could wait. Everything could wait, because what he wanted was *her* in his life. And he made up his mind right there that he would do whatever it took to get her into his life. His life and his children's lives. He wasn't going to let her go. She was already too important to him to take any chances.

Driving the wagon back to the hotel, he picked up his children and drove home, with Lindy still on his mind.

CHAPTER TWENTY

AFTER LINDY KISSED Cody good night, he said, "Mommy, I need to talk to you."

Lindy nodded and sat down on the bed. "Yes, Cody, what is it, darling?"

"Mommy, Amy and I were holding hands under the table."

Lindy laughed. "That's okay. Do you like her?"

"I love her, Mommy, I really love her. But, I don't want to hit her. Ever."

Lindy blinked. For a second, she didn't know what to say. Then she realized that all Cody had seen of a relationship between two people was violence. He had been brought up with *violence*. The thought bothered her. "Honey, not all men beat women. Your father is a bad man. Good men don't hit women."

"I asked Amy if her father ever hit her or her brothers."

"What did she say?" asked Lindy, wondering herself.

"She said that he had never hit any of them. So I guess then, that he is a good man."

Lindy nodded. "Yes, Cody, exactly. I'm sorry I stayed

with your father so long that you had to see all that violence. I'm so sorry." She leaned down and put her face next to his. "And I'm so sorry that he hit you, shoved you, and treated you badly. I promise you, that will never happen again."

"Okay, Mommy. I'm tired now. G'night." And he turned over and fell asleep.

Lindy, though, was visibly upset. Her hands were shaking. Rachel and Nick had already retired to the bedroom, and Oscar and Jamie were in the living room already sleeping, so she walked into the kitchen and sat down alone. Blissfully alone.

The conversation with Cody bothered her, but there was nothing she could do about it now. The damage had been done, and she would keep her promise to Cody. She would never again allow herself into a situation where either of them were abused. And now, she had to let it go. That part of her life—and Cody's—was over for good. Her whole life with Ray was a hundred years away right now, and they were safe here. And here is where they would stay. Safe.

But she had something else to think about—Brian. And she had no idea *what* to think. He hadn't taken his eyes off her all evening until his kids got into the food fight. After he had picked up all the errant peas, he wouldn't make eye contact at all. What was that about? The food fight certainly wasn't *her* fault. She was an innocent bystander.

Maybe he just felt embarrassed for his kids. Maybe he had wanted to make a good impression, and he felt like they had messed it up for him. That's what she was going to believe, anyway. Lindy wasn't going to take the blame for other people's actions. She did that too long with

Ray, so not now. It was *his* embarrassment, and it had nothing to do with her. Period. And besides, he did glance up when she hesitated to answer Eliza's question about eating there again the following night. So he was either interested or hoping that she'd say no! Lindy straightened up, put her shoulders back, and decided that he was interested and hoping that she'd say yes. And she was going with that.

Standing up, she reached over and turned off the flickering lantern. It was a battery operated lantern that looked like a real flame. It was to fool the neighbors into thinking that they were using candles. Apparently, all the twenty-first-century people who lived here used that deception and other similar ones.

It was funny how all these people moved into nineteenth-century Red Bluff, bringing with them flickering lanterns, composting toilets, and solar operated refrigerators. And since they mostly hung out together, nobody else was the wiser. She liked it here, in the past. She felt safe here. Although she'd never been much of a horseback rider, she could see herself getting a horse here some day, and maybe one for Cody, too. That would be good. What a life. And she didn't have to work for a living because of the way they exchanged money!

Oh! That reminded her. She had to start work the following day. It was just for something to do during the day when Cody was at school, but still, it was a job, and she had to be responsible. After getting undressed, she slipped into bed next to Cody, pulled the covers over her, and fell asleep.

When she awoke in the morning, she awoke with fresh memories of sweet dreams involving Brian. They had been dancing to an old-time melody, and he was looking into her eyes as if he were in love with her. And she was wildly, passionately in love with him. What a great dream, and one that she hoped would someday come true.

Lindy lay lounging in bed until she heard Rachel call from the other room, "Lindy! Don't forget you have to work today!" Then she jumped out of bed, waking Cody.

"Mommy?"

"It's okay, Cody. Mommy has to go to work today. You're going, too!" Then she said to Rachel, "I never asked Eliza about Cody. Do you think she'd mind if he stayed there at work with me? I think I've imposed on you enough."

"It would be no imposition to have him with the two boys, Lindy, really. But my guess is that Brian's kids will be at the hotel today while he goes *there* with Nick and Ryan. So Cody should be fine there. If not, just call me, and I'll come get him. Oh. That's right. You see? I've been here a year, and I still forget there are no phones yet! I hope they arrive soon, even if they are the old-fashioned kind!"

After they had finished eating breakfast, Rachel suggested that they walk over to the schoolhouse, since it was across the street and they still had time. Lindy and Cody walked across the street hand-in-hand next to Rachel. Oscar and Jamie held hands, but ran across the street. When they walked up to the schoolhouse, Lindy didn't know what to expect. It was a one room schoolhouse, as Rachel had told her, but when Lindy saw the chair-desks, she burst out laughing. They were from the twenty-first century!

"Don't let Josiah catch you laughing! He allowed Nick to bring these here—actually he didn't see them until

84

after they were here—but he allowed it because Nick convinced him that when Milo comes to school these chair-desks will make it easier for him to learn."

"I didn't think Josiah would be that gullible!" said Lindy, watching Oscar, Jamie, and Cody chase each other around the room.

"Well, it's not so much that he's gullible, but enough people have been on him to ease up a little on keeping the twenty-first century out of town. So, I think he's getting the hint."

"I better get off to work now." Lindy looked around the room and saw Cody running up and down with Rachel's two boys. He seemed perfectly at ease. "Cody, come on. Mommy has to go to work."

"Can't I stay here with Jamie and Oscar? Please, Mom, please?"

"Sorry, Cody, you have to come with me. But you can probably play with Willie, Archie, and Amy over at the hotel."

"*Amy?*" he asked and walked slowly toward her.

"Yup, come on!" She put out her hand, and he took it. "See ya later, Rachel!"

As they walked away, Lindy realized how easily Cody seemed to fit in here—like he was born to it. Part of it, she was sure, was that he felt safe here. Ray couldn't reach us here a hundred years in the past, she thought. They had finally found a place where they were completely free of him. Safe at last.

CHAPTER TWENTY-ONE

When Brian drove the wagon into town early in the morning, he had parked it in front of the general store in case Ryan had to load something to take *there*. And Brian and the children had walked over to the hotel, so he could get them settled in with Ma, before he had to leave. Now, he saw through the window that Ryan and Nick had parked the wagon in front of the hotel to pick him up. Brian stepped out of the hotel and was about to hop into the wagon when he noticed Lindy walking up the street with Cody. She was smiling and looking peaceful. His heart melted at the sight of her, and all he wanted to do was hold her in his arms. She hadn't noticed him yet, so he walked to meet her.

Cody saw him first. He said a quick "Hi" to Brian, and then said, "Mommy, can I go inside now?"

She nodded, looked up, and saw him. Cody ran into the hotel.

"Lindy!" He gently took both of her hands and squeezed them. "I'm so happy to see you. Sorry about what happened last night. I was never so embarrassed in my life! I'm so glad you said you'd come to supper again tonight so we can try again."

She smiled, cocked her head to one side, and said, "Yes, Brian, I'm glad, too."

"Come on, Brian!" called Nick from the wagon.

"I have to run, but I'll see you later, right?"

"Yes, Brian, I'll see you later." She smiled at him again.

He jumped into the wagon beside Nick and turned around. She was still watching him. "What are you doing here so early this morning?" he asked before the wagon had pulled away.

"Working!"

And then Dolly moved forward, Brian waved at Lindy, and he realized that his journey to a new and different world had just begun. He turned around a couple more times, but she had already gone inside.

"So you like her, huh?" asked Ryan.

"Yup, I do. I like her a lot," said Brian.

"Maybe we could go out on a triple date. Go out to dinner *there*, maybe go to a movie," said Ryan.

"I don't think Lindy wants to return *there* at all," said Nick. "She's too afraid that her ex-husband might find her. And if he happened to follow her back here, that would be horrible—for all of us."

"No, I think a conventional nineteenth-century courtship will be fine for me. I'm excited to see where y'all come from, but *this* is my home," said Brian. "But what's a triple date?"

"Later, dude," said Nick.

Brian looked around. "All right. Does it really only take an hour to get there?"

"No, not even an hour. We'll get to the cave soon, and it's not far after that," Nick said. "How was Josiah's house?"

"Oh! It was so comfortable being able to stretch out like that. The boys have their own room, and Amy sleeps on the couch in a sleeping sack."

Nick and Ryan laughed. "Sleeping bag, Brian, sleeping bag! If you're going to hang with twenty-first-century people, you have to learn the vernacular."

"Yeah, sleeping bag, all right. Anyway, it was incredibly comfortable, and I still can't believe that Josiah and Jenna are letting us use their house while they stay at the hotel."

"They stayed there when Jenna was in her late pregnancy. It was before I moved here and became deputy, so Josiah had to stay in town in case anyone needed him. And he didn't want Jenna staying out at the ranch all alone, in case she needed him. So they've stayed in that room before and were very comfortable there. Did you know that your folks upgraded that room just so they *could* stay there?" asked Nick.

"No, but I do remember that it used to be a storage room when I left."

"Ah, here we are, Brian. The cave." Ryan moved Dolly easily into the cave.

"At what point in the cave does it start being the twenty-first century?" asked Brian.

"No one knows. No one has tested it," said Nick.

"What's that?" asked Brian. He saw a large piece of metal that looked like it might be a fence.

"It's a piece of a fence panel," said Ryan. "Ask Josiah or Jenna to tell you that story about how they caught the cattle rustler. A guy from the twenty-first century stole cattle from the nineteenth century and sold them for a huge profit in the twenty-first. The thing is, even if he paid full price for the cattle here, he still could have made a fortune. But he got greedy. Anyway, it's a good story. And the reason we keep that fence panel there is to remind us that we in the nineteenth century are still vulnerable to anyone discovering the cave."

"Yeah, that makes sense." When they emerged from the cave, Brian looked around and nothing looked any different. "Everything looks the same!"

"Wait until we get to town, then nothing will look the same. Except the mountains. They'll always be right there." Ryan pointed toward the red-colored mountains that gave Red Bluff its name.

"They are the same! Exactly the same. Wow."

A few minutes later, Nick took the reins while Ryan got out and opened and closed the gates after the wagon went through. Soon, they were parked beside a big barn. When they released Dolly, she walked into the barn and into an empty stall all by herself. She started pawing at the empty food trough.

"Easy, girl. Here's a little hay to keep you until we get back. And some water." After giving her the hay, Ryan petted her on the head and said, "Let's go see if Zack and Madison are home. Nick, do you have the money bags?"

Nick walked back outside to the wagon, and when he returned, he carried two medium-sized canvas sacks. He handed one to Brian. "Feel how heavy it is. Josiah brought these over this morning. It's all the coins that Granny collected for you. This is all your money!"

Brian took the bag, which weighed several pounds. When he shook it, he could hear the metal coins inside. He didn't know how much was in there, but even without the fancy exchange that they talked about, he thought it was enough for him to build his own place.

They walked to the house, which looked different because no logs showed, and Ryan knocked on the door. They waited a few minutes, and Ryan and Nick looked around. "Both vehicles are here."

Brian had been too busy with the canvas sack full of money to look at anything but the house, so he hadn't noticed what they called vehicles until they were mentioned. They were bigger than a wagon, but not as big as a stagecoach. "Can I ride in one of those?"

"We will, soon," said Ryan. He put his hand on the handle and turned. It didn't turn. "That's curious. They've never locked the door before." Then he knocked again and pushed a button beside the door that made a bell sound inside. "That's called a doorbell, Brian."

Brian heard a small clunking sound, and the door swung open. He saw a young man there with a gun belt around his waist—nothing unusual in his time.

But Ryan and Nick both stood outside without entering, and Nick said, "You're wearing a *gun* belt!"

"Yeah, come on in. I'll tell you why."

Ryan made the introductions, and Brian learned that this was Zack. He had been born in the nineteenth century, but came here to live with Madison and to go to college. Zack loved it in the twenty-first century and wasn't planning to return to the nineteenth.

"So Lindy's ex-husband came here while we were taking her there, and he pushed over some lamps. If he comes back, we want to be prepared. So we always lock the doors now. But we had keys made for everybody. I'll give them to you to distribute to whoever needs them."

"What makes you think that it was her ex-husband? Couldn't it be just random?"

"No, it wasn't random," said a woman who walked into the room from the back. "Hi. I'm Madison. You must be Brian." She stuck out her hand to shake his. Then she pulled something from behind her back. "Look what he did to Cody's toy. It was definitely him." She held out the toy, and it was in two pieces, looking like someone had chopped its head off. "He used the meat cleaver in the kitchen."

"That guy is scary. To do this to a kid's toy—his own kid!" Nick shook his head. "Oh, hey, Zack. These are from Granny for Brian." Nick put the two bags of coins on the sofa. "Whenever you can get around to it would be great. Brian wants to buy some land, and I'm going to help him build his own place. In exchange, he's going to help me build a second story over the jailhouse!"

"Sounds like a deal! Granny had told me she would have a lot to exchange, so Madison and I drove to the city south of town a couple of times so I already have a large amount of old coins available. You're going shopping, right? I'll try to have the exchange done before you get back."

Brian smiled. These people from the twenty-first century were so kind and generous. And if Zack did have money saved already to exchange for him, then maybe he could even buy the land the following day! His own land! Even if they wouldn't build on it any time soon, it would still be his. Madison's words interrupted his thoughts.

"Should we show him the miracles of twenty-first-century living?" she asked.

"No, not yet. We have a lot to do today," Ryan said. "Zack, just show him the bathroom."

91

CHAPTER TWENTY-TWO

WHEN LINDY WALKED into the hotel, she expected to see the children running around. But instead, she found the four of them sitting at a table in the restaurant talking to Eliza. No one else was around. Standing in the doorway, she heard what Eliza said.

"Now remember, running around is what children do, and I'm completely all right with that. But running around and making a lot of noise when there are strangers here, or when people are trying to eat, is not all right. There are times to run around and times to behave. You're all old enough to know the difference. Right?"

All the children nodded their heads, and Eliza continued. "You're all welcome to go play now, but you must be aware of what's going on around you. If one of you notices customers in the restaurant, he or she will tell the others. Is that understood?" They all nodded again. "So are there any customers in the restaurant right now?" The children shook their heads. "Then you can go run around and play! Go on now!"

The kids jumped up and ran off, albeit quietly, and

Eliza walked up to where Lindy stood. "Good morning! You're right on time!"

"I hope Cody wasn't a bother. I'm sorry. I didn't know if I should bring him or not—"

"He's been fine—hasn't made any more noise than the rest of them! Come on over to the front desk, let me show you how we do things around here."

For the next hour, Eliza went over everything at the front desk, the restaurant, and the kitchen. Since Granny and Edward did a lot of the cooking, and now they wanted to retire, Eliza would need more help in the kitchen. When she asked if Lindy was willing to learn that, Lindy agreed willingly. She was happy to have a job where everyone was kind and friendly. She'd do anything that was asked of her.

When they finished all the instructions, Eliza said, "I don't expect much to be happening for quite a while. You're welcome to walk around town, go home, or whatever for an hour or two. Go ahead, check out the town."

Lindy didn't know what to do. She hadn't expected any time off, except maybe for lunch, and she had figured she would stay there and eat. So she didn't know what to do. But when Jenna and baby Milo came out of their room a minute later, followed by her dog, Jet, it all worked out. Eliza had retreated into her living area, no one else was around, so Jenna invited her into the restaurant to talk.

"Would you like me to get us both a cup of coffee?" asked Lindy.

"Yeah, that would be great." Jenna sat down holding a sleepy Milo with his head on her shoulder. Jet lay down at her feet.

After Lindy brought the coffee and sat down, Jenna

asked, "How do you like it here so far?"

"I love it. Everyone here is so kind and helpful." Lindy looked down. "And of course, there's that other little thing that I feel safe here."

"I'd say that's a big thing. Your lip seems to be healing well."

"At least it doesn't look so big anymore! Nothing like a fat lip to draw attention to yourself!" They both laughed. "How long have you lived here, Jenna?"

"It's been two years since I stumbled through the cave and discovered this place. It didn't take long to fall in love with Josiah and decide to move here—although it took longer to persuade *him* that me coming from the twenty-first century didn't mean that I wasn't suitable for him. I think at first, he was scared of me." Jenna looked at her. "But it doesn't sound like Brian is afraid of you at all."

Lindy coughed and laughed. "Boy, this *is* a small town!"

"Josiah told me about supper last night—you know, the food fight and all. And he also told me—I probably shouldn't tell you this, but maybe you need to hear it— that Brian likes you."

Lindy nodded. "I like him, too. A lot. We're coming to dinner—er, supper—here again tonight. You know, to make up for last night. And tonight will be without the kids!"

"That's probably a good idea—considering! So, I know this is jumping ahead at this point, but if Brian asked you to marry him, would you consider staying here?"

"Oh, there's no question. Regardless of what happens with Brian, I'll never go back there. I'm safe here. *We're* safe here. I'm not going back."

"Yes, it is safe here. My first time here, Josiah was out of town and his drunk deputy was not taking care of business. I met a cowboy in the saloon who was cute"—Jenna shrugged and smiled—"and next thing you know he was out in front involved in a gunfight! I thought it was a movie set, so I clapped my hands and acted like an idiot, until I leaned down to help the guy up. There was real blood on him! And he was dead! I didn't think I'd ever return here, but, you know Sarah? Anyway, Sarah wanted to come to sing in the saloon, so I reluctantly came back, got to know Josiah, and the rest is history!"

"Wow! What a story!" Lindy set her cup of coffee on the table.

"Yeah, since then, everything's been real quiet. Josiah keeps a tight rein so none of that goes on now. Everything's been so calm and peaceful here that Josiah has considered not wearing a gun any more, but he thought maybe someone would try to take advantage of that, so he's reluctantly kept it on."

"Where is Josiah? By the way, that was sure sweet of him to serve us last night. He looked so cute in that apron!"

"Oh, he enjoyed it. He's at the office today, because Nick went to *town* with Ryan and Brian."

"That's Brian's first time there, right?"

"Yes, his first time." Jenna nodded.

"Well, he'll have a good time seeing everything there is to see." Then a dark thought crossed her mind. Ray was there. Mean, miserable Ray. And that's where Brian was going. "I hope he stays safe over there," she said quietly.

CHAPTER TWENTY-THREE

BRIAN HAD THOUGHT the inside necessary, as he called it
—though it was really called a composting toilet—was
amazing, but the bathroom that Zack had showed him
was incredible! The toilet had water to flush the waste
away, so there was no smell at all! And a bathtub and
what Zack called a shower, where water came from a
little spout at the top and sprayed all over you. Zack said
it was refreshing and that he loved it, but Brian wasn't so
sure.

"Come on, Brian," Nick called out. "Time's a
wasting!"

Ryan had already left while Brian was in the
bathroom. Nick said they would be taking separate vehicles because of all the different places they had to go. So
Brian climbed into what Nick had said was a truck, and
then buckled his seat belt as Nick showed him.

When Nick drove off, Brian kept asking, "Can't you go
any faster? This must go faster!"

"Whoa, Brian, whoa. Yes, it goes faster, but there are
speed limits here. See the signs?"

"Oh, all right. Where are we going first?"

"College. I know it's closed today, but sometimes they put their extras out in the breezeway between buildings. Ah, yes, there's some of what I'm looking for." Nick parked the truck, and they both got out of the vehicle.

"What do you need these for?" asked Brian.

"Because it has come to my attention that there are several new kids in town," said Nick, holding onto a chair-desk in each hand.

Brian grabbed two of them and followed Nick to the truck. "Oh. Oh! You mean my three and Cody!"

"Yup. The schoolhouse needs two more to accommodate everybody, and I'll get a couple of extra and keep them in my horse trailer." Nick arranged them in the back of the truck and then said, "Come on, let's go. The next place is close."

Brian watched the buildings as they drove past them. So many of them, and so many different kinds. He'd been in cities before, but nothing like this. And none of the streets here were dirt. The pavement underneath the truck's wheels was smooth. It was all so different. He liked seeing everything, but it wasn't somewhere that he'd ever like to live.

Nick pulled in front of a store that said *Humane Society Thrift Store*. There were clothes and somewhat familiar objects in the front window.

"What's in here?" Brian asked.

"Clothes for your beloved. Rachel said that Lindy didn't know jeans weren't allowed where she was going, so she didn't bring anything that was suitable. She's been wearing Rachel's clothes."

"Oh! Can I help you pick something out, then?"

"Dude, you can do all the picking out!" said Nick, holding the door open for Brian.

97

Brian looked carefully at all the skirts, noting that many would not be appropriate in the nineteenth century. Finally he picked one skirt out. "This is it, Nick. This is the one."

"Just one?" asked Nick. "Lindy's a twenty-first-century girl. She'll need more than one skirt. Go ahead and pick out four or five, and then some blouses, too."

Half an hour later, Brian walked out of the thrift store with six skirts, seven blouses, and one dress for Lindy, and two pairs of jeans, and three shirts for himself, since he had left most of his clothes in Virginia. He also bought a few items of clothes for the children, and a doll for Amy.

Next stop on their list was the lumber store, to get some lumber for the second story of the sheriff's office. They also bought a few items that Brian would need when they built his house, like hinges for the doors, window casements, a shovel, and some other building apparatus. And Nick bought something called a chain saw that he said would help with cutting down trees on Brian's new land. Brian didn't understand why they would need the chain saw, though, since he bought two other reliable two-man saws, and a couple of smaller ones. But he trusted Nick, so he shrugged his shoulders and nodded when Nick said what he was buying. Nick also bought something called a gas can that Brian had no idea what it was used for.

After taking the chair-desks out of the back and then rearranging all the lumber and putting the small items inside, Nick and Brian climbed back into the truck. "One last stop," said Nick, "a gas station. I might as well fill up my truck as long as I'm here."

They stopped in front of several tall rectangular objects that Nick called gas pumps. Nick slid a little card into the machine and then pumped fluid into his truck. He said that's what it takes to make them run. Then he pumped some of the fluid into the gas can and said it was for the chain saw. He used the gas can to fill the chain saw because it had a narrow spout, and then he refilled the gas can. Nick mentioned that they might have to come back and get more gas depending on how many trees they needed to cut down on Brian's land.

As they drove away from the gas station, Nick looked at something on his truck that he said told the time. It confused Brian because it didn't have a face, but Nick showed him how to read it. "We still have some time before we meet Ryan. Are you hungry?"

"Not really," said Brian. "Ma gave us all a huge breakfast this morning. I can probably go until supper tonight."

"How about ice cream?" asked Nick, smiling.

"Ice cream? Yeah! I have room for that!"

When they arrived at the ice cream parlor, Nick called it, they walked inside, and Brian was astounded at all the choices. He had no idea what most of the flavors were because they had names that he didn't recognize, so he looked at all of them, and choose three for a triple decker. He chose Rocky Road, which he did recognize from the party the other night, and Cherry Jubilee, and Fudge Brownie Delite. Each layer of the cone was more delicious than the last. He couldn't believe the flavors and how great they tasted.

They drove back to the house. Ryan was already there and had the wagon loaded with all his stuff. Brian and Nick finished loading it with the lumber, the clothes, and two of the chair-desks. Ryan handed Brian one of the bags of coins. "This is some of the money that Zack exchanged. It should last you for a while. He wanted to keep some back for twenty-first-century money in case you wanted that. And he said that Granny had found some really valuable coins. Zack said there was one worth a hundred grand! A half dime, I think he said. Anyway, he didn't have enough to pay you everything, so he still owes you a lot more. They'll go back to the city again soon to get more."

"Great! I owe Nick some money. Is there enough there to buy my land?"

Ryan laughed. "Brian, there's enough here to buy the entire town, and Zack still has more for you! Let's get going."

They all climbed into the wagon and rode through the gates, with Brian opening and closing them this time, and then rode out onto the main trail. Brian felt so happy that he could barely contain himself. He had money to buy land, a friend who would help him build a house, and his eye on a woman whom he felt strongly about. Life couldn't have been any greater. Although he might not have felt so optimistic if he had known of the danger that lay ahead.

CHAPTER TWENTY-FOUR

RAY HAD SAT in the car parked behind a truck for most of every day since Lindy had disappeared. And finally, *finally* it had paid off. Three men walked out of the barn and into the house. He saw that the man of the house wore a gun belt to answer the door, but it didn't matter. Ray had already determined that the man and woman in the house were together. Crouching in the dark at their window, Ray had seen evidence of it the prior night. Of course, that didn't mean that the man would refuse a little on the side, so he wasn't free and clear of suspicion yet. But for now, Ray would let it go.

Using the binoculars, Ray had seen a wagon parked outside the barn. Perfect! A wagon would be much easier to follow than horses. His plan was coming together, and he couldn't be any happier. Thinking about the looks of the three men, he wondered which was the one involved with Lindy. Had any of them looked like Cody? Were any of them Cody's father, he wondered. No way to know, and it didn't matter anyway. It might have been one of Lindy's one night stands. He had plenty of them, so he knew that Lindy must have, too. Women were like

101

that. They just couldn't get enough, no matter how good their partner was.

That's what his mother had told him, and he believed her. He hated her, but he believed her. The day that she had told him that his father wasn't really his father, still annoyed him. Annoyed him? It made him furious! Ray had hated her for that and hated his father for not being his father. And he hated whoever *was* his real father, although his mother would never tell him. With all his might, he hit the dashboard with his fist, leaving four knuckle marks in it that were slow to disappear.

Lindy would pay for that. She'd pay for everything any woman had ever done to him, and she'd pay good.

Ray's thoughts had faded as one man came out of the house and drove away in a truck. Several minutes later, the other two left the house. They drove away in another truck. While he waited for them to return, he refined his plan. When they returned, he would remove the bike from the bicycle rack at the back of the car, and he would follow them at a respectable distance. Which was now, finally, what he was doing.

He had waited in the car for hours, then watched as they loaded the wagon, and watched as they drove the wagon through the first gate. Then he was on the bike and through a path that he had found on one of the days he had sat there. It would connect with the trail that they were on. No matter which way they went, he could follow them. Although when he had first come up with the idea, his plan was to use a motorbike, he realized that with the quiet ways of horses—or the wagon—the motorbike sound would be too noticeable. There would be plenty of time for that, later.

Hidden in the bushes, Ray watched as the wagon went

by with only a few creaks and groans and the conversations of the men. None of the men had seen him, although the horse snorted and whinnied as it went by. He did always have a way with animals—Ray laughed silently—he liked to hurt 'em, almost as much as he liked to hurt Lindy.

If she thought prison was going to change his ways, she should have thought again. It was an education! He had learned things in prison that he couldn't have learned anywhere else. And he had been a good student. And if she thought that he would get over his anger toward her while he was in there, she was sadly mistaken. It had only intensified. That day at the house when he had knocked her down, that was only the beginning.

The wagon had passed and the sound of voices had gone. Ray slowly pulled the bike out of the bushes and onto the trail. Not only could he see them in the distance, but the wagon tracks made an easy trail to follow. He was so lucky, and Lindy was so stupid, thinking he'd never find her. Oh, he'd find her all right, and he would make her sorry when he did. And he'd hurt her but good. What would hurt her the worst, though, was taking the boy from her. That made him smile.

The wagon tracks had disappeared before he realized it, so he had to backtrack to find them again. They went up the hill, zigging and zagging around trees, bushes, and rocks. Once he realized what to look for, the trail wasn't hard to follow, but the trail was too rough for the bike. After leaving the bike behind a bush, he followed the trail on foot, but he was completely surprised when he came to the cave. He didn't know there was a cave here.

Glancing at his watch, he nodded, hurried back down

the hill, pulled the bike up, and rode back the way he had come. His shift started in fifteen minutes. He'd be late, but he didn't care. He'd make up some stupid excuse that they would surely believe. They always did. And he'd return here later with the motorbike. He'd drive around and find her. And he'd take the boy away from her, because he knew that boy was the most important thing in the world to her—just like *he* had been— before the boy was born. And when Ray returned, he'd bring his gun.

CHAPTER TWENTY-FIVE

WHEN THE MEN returned, Lindy was in the middle of serving people in the restaurant. Brian had stuck his head in, waved to her, and then he and his children had left. So Cody was stuck with nothing to do, until Rachel showed up unexpectedly and took him home with her. The rest of the afternoon Lindy had kept busy, and by the end of the day, she felt tired. When it was time to leave, Eliza had said, "Sorry to have kept you so late. I didn't expect to be so busy today. Supper is in an hour! See you soon!"

Lindy walked home exhausted and sank into the sofa as soon as she got there. The three boys were playing a board game on the floor. Cody looked up briefly and said "Hi, Mom," and then went back to his game. It made Rachel smile, and then she closed her eyes to get at least a little rest before she had to leave.

Nick and Rachel were in the bedroom talking, but when they heard Cody say hello to her, they came out to see her. Rachel carried an armful of clothes. "Your new clothes, Madam," said Rachel, handing her the clothes.

That woke Lindy up. She looked through the clothes:

several blouses and several skirts, and one blue dress with white trim. They all looked like they would fit her perfectly, and she liked every one. "Wow! Thank you." Lindy looked up at Nick. "Thanks so much for getting them for me."

"Rachel told me to buy some clothes for you," explained Nick, "but Brian's the one who picked them out. And he said that he'd like you to wear the blue dress tonight."

Lindy felt overwhelmed. "Brian did? Really?" The tiredness had gotten to her, and this simple gesture of kindness made tears come to her eyes. She brushed them away, jumped up, and said, "I'm going to try everything on right now!"

When she stepped into her room, the bed beckoned, and she thought she'd lie down for a few minutes to rest her eyes before supper tonight. Her eyes rested and so did the rest of her, and when Rachel woke her up an hour later, Lindy said, "Oh, no! I'm late!" She threw the dress on, combed her hair, and from the bowl of water in her room, she sprinkled water on her face and then started out the door. It wasn't until she had crossed the street that she realized that Nick was following directly behind her. "Oh! Hi, Nick! What are you doing here?" Lindy said with her head half-turned and not slowing her pace at all.

"I'm coming to offer our services to Brian's kids." Nick took two quick strides and was even with her. Then he opened the door to the hotel.

Lindy walked in and ran directly into Brian. "Lindy!" He took both her hands in his. "I was so worried! I thought something had happened to you!"

She looked down. "I fell asleep, sorry."

He released her hands, put his arm around her, and squeezed her to him. "I'm just glad you're all right." Then he kissed her on the top of her head. "Hey, Nick. Thank you for escorting my girl here for me! I appreciate that."

"Actually, I was going to ask you if you'd like me to take your kids for you tonight. Do they play cards?"

"They love playing cards, and they're all good at it, too, even Amy. But be careful of Archie." He leaned over conspiratorially, "He'll look at your cards if he gets half a chance!"

Granny strode into the room with her arms crossed on her chest. "What's this I hear about you taking my grandchildren away?" she demanded.

"I was just inviting them over to the house to play cards and board games with my kids. Would that be all right with you, Granny?" Nick asked.

Granny uncrossed her arms, her eyes lit up, and she hugged Nick. "Thank you, Nick! I knew you were a good boy!" Then she turned around and returned to the restaurant, saying in a loud voice, "Old man! We have our evening free, big boy! Woohoo!"

Nick raised his eyebrows. "I thought she was going to hit me, but she hugged me, instead." That made Brian and Lindy laugh. Then Nick called into the restaurant, "Willie! Archie! Amy! Come on with me! Let's go play some cards!" The three kids ran to the door and followed Nick out, while waving to Brian as they went.

Brian crossed his arms over his chest. "Hrmmph! That's loyalty!"

Lindy looked into the restaurant and saw Josiah, Jenna, and the baby sitting at a table by the entrance, and she waved to them. Granny, Edward, and Samuel sat at a table closer to the kitchen. She motioned with her head. "Aren't they going to eat with us?"

Brian shook his head. "No. Just you and me!" He took her hand and led her into Eliza's dining room. Then he pulled out a chair for her to sit down.

"What service!" said Lindy.

Eliza walked out of the kitchen and put two serving platters on the table, one with fried chicken and the other with mashed potatoes on one side and peas on the other. "I thought the peas would be safe with you two. Enjoy!"

Lindy looked up at her. "I'm so sorry I'm late, Eliza! I fell asleep!"

"It's no wonder after how much I ran you around today! I didn't expect us to be so busy. No problem, though. Brian was worried sick that you weren't going to show after last night's, um, incident."

"Ah, no, here I am." She smiled at Brian across the table.

"You two kids enjoy yourselves, now." Eliza disappeared back into the kitchen.

Brian held the platter of chicken out to Lindy and smiled at her. After Lindy took two pieces of chicken, Brian took two, also, and held out the potatoes and peas to her. While she helped herself, Brian said, "We're finally alone so we can talk. I want to hear all about you!"

Lindy started by telling him how she had met and started dating Ray in her final year in high school. She told him that Ray had come from another school, and that she didn't find out until much later that he had gotten kicked out of the other school for beating up a kid from his class.

She and Ray had attended schools in the same town—

she to college, and he to a trade school—and continued dating. He had never shown any sign of abuse, except for yelling at her and throwing things. That changed when she was in college and thought she was pregnant. Ray exploded with anger and hit her right in the stomach. When Lindy said that, she saw Brian drop his fork and ball up his fists. But this was her story, so she continued. It turned out she hadn't been pregnant at all, and Ray had apologized profusely and bought her flowers and promised that he would never hit her again.

Shortly after that, they married, and she did get pregnant. At first, everything was fine, and they were both excited about a new baby. But when she told Ray that she couldn't go drinking with him because she was pregnant, he had slapped her *hard* across the face, walked out, and didn't return until the following day, stinking of alcohol and another woman's perfume. Lindy sighed and said that she probably should have left then, but didn't, and then Cody was born, so how could she leave with a new baby?

She glanced up at Brian who hadn't taken another bite of food and still had his hands balled into fists, and she thought that she was glad that Ray was there and Brian was here. She wouldn't want to see them together. Then she hurried to finish the story so Brian could relax.

"So I divorced him while he was in prison, and I thought that was the end of it, until he came to my house that day." Lindy shrugged. "And that's how I got here."

Brian didn't say anything for a while and then his fists relaxed. With one hand he picked up his fork, and with the other hand he reached across the table and squeezed one of her hands. "And I'm glad you're here. I want you to know that you'll always be safe with me. I'll protect you, and I'll never hurt you."

Lindy blinked the tears away and said, "I know, Brian. I know you'll never hurt me or Cody. You're a good, kind man." What she didn't say was that he was a good, kind man whom she would like to marry some day.

CHAPTER TWENTY-SIX

RAY'S HANDS FELT sweaty with excitement as he rode the motorbike slowly along the trail that he remembered from the afternoon. Some of the wagon tracks were still there, although other horses had been through obscuring most of them. He had *obtained* the motor bike the same way that he had *obtained* the bicycle. Another lesson from his days in prison: always be aware of what's around you because some day you may need some of what you notice. When he found himself in need of a bicycle and a motorbike, he knew exactly where to get them. And, bonus! He knew how to hot wire the motorcycle. Who said that prison was a dead end? Look at all he had learned! Ray laughed at the irony of it all.

When he had gone to work that afternoon—late—it turned out that they didn't believe his lame excuse after all. What was so hard to believe about having two flat tires? So they had fired him. Oh, well. It was a crummy job anyway. He'd find something much better with more pay. That was one thing that he'd never had a problem doing—finding a job. Of course, it was a little more difficult now that he had the label of *ex-con* attached to him—thanks to *her*. But he wasn't concerned. The right job would come to him. It always did.

And *her*. He could hardly wait to get to her and rough her up a bit. And he might as well take her, too. There was no reason not to. She was still his wife, after all. Divorce? He not only didn't believe in divorce, but *he* had never signed any papers. It wasn't *his* divorce. She was still his wife, and he could take her any time he wanted. And he wanted to, now. He'd mess her up some first, then force himself on her, and then finish the job, leaving just enough life in her to be torn up when he took the boy away. He rubbed his hands on his pants to get the sweat off them, but he hit a dip in the dirt trail and had to grab the bike fast to keep from losing control. Oh! He'd get her for that!

Although he would have liked to go faster to get to her sooner, he wasn't sure where the turn-off trail was to the cave. If he recalled correctly, it wasn't that clearly marked. He didn't want to miss it this time. It came upon him sooner than he expected. Trying to get the motor-bike up the trail, around the bushes and trees and avoiding the rocks didn't work too well. The bike hit a big rock twice, and he went down. The second time his knee hit a rock, and he screamed in agony before getting up and kicking the bike several times and then kicking the rock once for good measure. He left the bike where it lay, and it wasn't until he took a few steps forward that he realized that he was missing something.

The gun! He walked back to find it by the rock that he hit his knee on. After picking it up, he looked at it carefully to make sure it wasn't damaged. Ray would have liked to shoot it to make sure it worked, but he didn't want anyone to know he was coming. No, it looked fine, he'd have to trust that it would work if he needed it. He didn't anticipate needing it; he expected her not to be in any condition to complain when he walked away with the boy, but just in case, he had it. And maybe he'd hit her in the face with it a time or two. He'd like the feel of that in his hand. Sticking it behind him in the waistband of his pants, he kept walking up the hill.

A few minutes later, he reached the cave and slowly walked through it. Mid-cave, he looked up and saw the late afternoon light filtering in through a narrow opening. Another minute passed, and he walked out of the cave. He looked around and had no idea where he was. No horses had walked over these wagon tracks, so it was easy to follow them through to the road—a dirt road. And there it was—the most curious thing: an old wooden sign that said *Red Bluff*.

CHAPTER TWENTY-SEVEN

BRIAN ATE A few bites of food trying to catch up, since he hadn't eaten during Lindy's story. He saw that she had gotten emotional when he said he'd protect her, so he wanted to let her relax before going on. But then Lindy had said, "Now you tell me about yourself."

So he explained how he and his brother William—Willie was named after him—had insisted on going to fight in the Civil War. They were in one of the first battles in Virginia. William was shot down right next to him, and then he had gotten hit in the head with a bullet. It was a glancing blow, but he was unconscious for he didn't know how long. Then he told her briefly about Bella taking care of him and them marrying and her getting sick and dying. He had a difficult time telling the story without becoming emotional himself, so he moved quickly on to when Ma and Pa showed up at the farm, and described their trip back here.

Brian looked up at her and reached out and stroked her hand. "We've both been through a lot, haven't we?" She smiled back at him and nodded, and they were lost in the moment staring into each other's eyes, when someone stomped into the room.

"Well, isn't this cozy?" said a man standing in the doorway with his hands on his hips.

When Lindy froze, turned, and cowered, Brian knew exactly who it was, so he stood up. "What do you want? You don't belong here."

"Neither does she!" the man said and walked forward a few paces. He pointed at Lindy. "That's my wife you're being all cozy with."

Without emotion, Lindy said, "We're divorced, Ray. I haven't been your wife for a year."

"I never signed any papers! As far as I'm concerned, we're still married"—Ray glanced at Brian and smile—"and I expect *her* to perform her wifely duties." He pulled a gun out from behind his back and waved it at Brian. "So you get away from her, and we'll get along fine. And then I want to find that boy of hers. I'm taking him back with me."

Brian took two swift paces which placed him in front of Lindy. "You'll do no such thing. Leave us alone, now! Go back to where you belong!"

Ray narrowed his eyes and lifted the gun, and then Brian saw Josiah come up behind him.

"Put down the gun, big guy. My gun is bigger, and I swear I'll blow you away if you don't drop it right now. In this town, we have what we call Frontier Justice, and if I blew you away, everyone would just cheer me on. Put it down, now!"

Brian could see Ray's face screwing up with anger and his hand shaking, but after a second's hesitation, he put the gun down. He could hear Lindy crying softly behind him.

"Now kick it away, nice and gentle like," said Josiah.

115

After Ray kicked the gun away, Josiah said, "Put your hands behind you, slow and easy."

Ray's fists clenched and unclenched, but finally he thrust his arms behind him. Josiah cuffed him and turned him around. Then Nick walked in carrying a rifle. "What do we have here?" asked Nick.

"I haven't done anything wrong!" said Ray.

"A felon with a gun? Dude, I think that's slightly against the law," said Nick.

"What are we going to do with him now?" asked Josiah. "We can't throw him in jail *here*."

"I could take him back *there* and turn him in, but I think that would be too difficult to explain."

"Dang it all," said Josiah. "You mean we're going to have to let him go?"

"It's up to you, Josiah, but I don't see any way around it." He poked at Ray with the gun. "Of course, if he comes back here, then we could kill him—"

"Come on, let's get him out of here. We'll walk him to the cave," said Josiah. Turning around he said, "Brian, did you want to come with us?"

"Brian, no, please," said Lindy.

He put his hand on her shoulder. "This is something I have to do, Lindy. I'll be back shortly." Then he followed Ray, Nick, and Josiah out of the hotel. "Should I get the wagon, Josiah?"

"That's a great idea, Brian. That way we won't have to smell the stench of this no-account for so long. Hurry, though."

Brian ran all the way to the livery and had Dolly trot back to the hotel. Josiah still had his gun pointed at Ray, and Nick still had his rifle pointed at him. The sight made Brian shiver.

After he had recovered from the bullet wound to his head, he had sworn never to take up a gun again. The remembrance of shooting men and boys—many younger than himself—still haunted him. But he understood it was necessary with Ray.

"You drive, Brian, and we'll sit in the back with this piece of garbage." Josiah climbed in first, followed by Ray, who stumbled and fell head first into the bed of the wagon, and then Nick climbed in.

"We're taking you back where you came from instead of letting you rot in our jail here. But we don't ever want to see you back," said Josiah.

"Oh, you'll never *see* me, that's for sure," said Ray, cryptically.

Brian stopped Dolly at the mouth of the cave. "Should I go through, or will we let him off here?"

"He can walk," said Josiah. "Get out!"

Ray tumbled out of the wagon and struggled to stand up. "Are you going to keep these cuffs on me?"

"I'd like to, but no. Turn around."

When Josiah unlocked the cuffs, Ray turned around and rubbed his wrists. "I won't forget any of this." He squinted his eyes at Josiah. Then he pointed at Brian. "And don't think that you're getting off scot-free after stealing my woman!"

"Get out of here, you loser!" Josiah gave him a shove. Ray scowled and started walking through the cave, still rubbing his wrists. "Don't *ever* come back here," yelled Josiah after him.

"I'm following until he leaves on the other side," said Nick. "We can't watch after he makes the little turn inside there."

"Good idea," said Josiah.

117

Brian and Josiah watched until Ray and then Nick disappeared at the curve in the cave. Several minutes later, Nick walked back. "I watched until he walked down the hill. Then I heard a motorcycle start up and drive away. Luckily, he couldn't get it up the hill. A motorcycle coming through town would have had people talking!"

"I think we got off easy," said Josiah. "If Sarah at the saloon hadn't noticed that he paid for his drink with a new coin and then guessed who he was, everything might have turned out much worse."

Brian shook his head. "He might have shot me or Lindy or both of us. And Cody——"

Josiah and Nick climbed onto the seat beside him. "It's all right, Brian. None of that happened. We got lucky this time, but we can't take any more chances. The guy is dangerous. Nick, we'll need to have a guard posted at the cave night and day. We can talk about it tomorrow, but tonight——"

"I'll take first watch, Josiah. No worries."

"I don't think he'll be coming back this evening, so go ahead on home and get what you need," said Josiah.

Brian swallowed hard. He knew that volunteering for guard duty meant carrying a gun and possibly using it. But Lindy was his responsibility—at least he felt like she was. "I'll put in my time, too. But I'll need to get a gun. I don't have one—anymore." Then he brightened. "I can have *Ray's* gun!"

Josiah shook his head. "No. Too twenty-first century. We'll talk about it tomorrow, Brian. Tonight, you need to go comfort Lindy. I think she'll need it." Josiah motioned with his head toward Dolly. "Let's go back now."

Brian shook the reins, turned Dolly around, and headed back to town.

CHAPTER TWENTY-EIGHT

WHEN THE MEN walked out, Lindy curled into herself with her hands over her face, crying hysterically. She couldn't believe what had just happened. Lindy thought she was *safe* here! Her mistake. Now, not only was she in danger, but she had endangered *everyone* in town with her troubles.

Sarah entered the room and rushed over to Lindy, patting her on the back. "It's okay, Lindy. They took him away. Everything will be okay."

Lindy looked up at her with a tear-stained face. "No, Sarah. Nothing will be okay. Ray knows I'm here. I'm not safe here and neither is anyone else. I have to leave!"

Eliza walked out of the kitchen, oblivious to what had just gone on. "Here's dessert for—" She looked around. "Where's Brian? What's going on?"

"Ray came, and Josiah and Nick—and Brian—took him away," Lindy squeaked out and began crying all over again.

"What?" asked Eliza, putting the chocolate cake and ice cream on the table.

Lindy couldn't speak, but she felt motion from Sarah

and assumed that she had shaken her head at Eliza, because Eliza didn't say another word, just put her hand on Lindy's shoulder for support.

A few minutes later, Lindy struggled to stand up. "I need to go back to the house."

Sarah helped her stand. "I'll walk you down there, Lindy."

They walked to the doorway, with Sarah's arm around Lindy supporting her. Lindy turned her head and looked back into the room. "I'm afraid I can't work tomorrow."

Eliza nodded. "I understand, dear."

As they headed toward Rachel and Nick's house on the corner, Lindy began crying again. "I still can't believe that it happened. He came *here* to get to me—and Cody! I have to leave and find someplace new that's safe. Someplace where he'll never find me."

Sarah, still with her arm around Lindy's shoulder, took her hand. "Lindy, listen. You're still in shock after what's just happened. When you settle down, you'll be fine."

Lindy knew that she wouldn't be fine, but she wasn't going to argue with Sarah. If it wasn't for Sarah noticing Ray, everything could have turned out much differently. She shuddered with the thought. Sarah had said that she noticed Ray right off when he walked into the saloon. And she said it wasn't his clothing, but his attitude—the attitude of a troublemaker. When she had seen him pay Matthew with a new coin, she waited to see what he was going to do, then she followed him over to the hotel and immediately told Josiah, who was in the restaurant. What if Josiah hadn't been in the restaurant? What then? It was too horrible to think about.

"Here we are," said Sarah. "Rachel will take care of you now."

"Thanks so much, Sarah. Thanks for walking me home, and I can never thank you enough for noticing Ray." Lindy's tears started afresh. She put her hand on the door handle, then turned back to Sarah. "Can you do me one more huge favor? Can you come in for a minute and tell Rachel what happened? If I have to retell it, I'll break down again."

As they walked through the doorway, Lindy whispered, "But not in front of the kids." Lindy went straight to her bedroom, and when Cody, sitting on the floor with Rachel and the other children, said, "Hi, Mom!" Lindy tried her best to say "hello" in a normal voice. Then she closed the door gently behind her, threw herself on the bed, and the heaving sobs began, with Lindy muffling them with the pillow. She could hear voices through the door, and then she heard the front door open and close. Rachel knows. And now that she knows that Lindy's problems had endangered her own husband, Rachel might not be so keen on allowing her to stay at their house. Friendship was one thing, but this was something else entirely.

Every time Lindy's sobs gave way to normal breathing, she remembered the incident with Ray so vividly that she could almost reach out and touch him. And then the sobs would return, and she'd bury her face in the pillow again to keep from disturbing anyone. She didn't want Cody to know that Ray had found them here, and she especially didn't want him to know that Ray had wanted to take him back with him. Cody was already terrified of Ray. No telling what would happen if he found out about that.

Lindy shuddered. There was only one right thing to do. She had to leave the old Red Bluff. Ray *would* return, there was no doubt about that. And she and Cody had to be long gone when he did. It was the only choice that she had. She had no idea where she could go to get away from him, but she'd figure it out. They'd leave tomorrow.

CHAPTER TWENTY-NINE

NICK AND JOSIAH talked about what they were going to do and how they were going to handle it, but Brian didn't hear a word. All he could think about was what Josiah said: "*Tonight, you need to go comfort Lindy.*" Josiah said it as if Lindy already belonged to Brian. The thought gave Brian a funny feeling in his stomach, until he realized what it was. That was exactly what he wanted. He wanted Lindy to belong to him. They would be one big family. He and Lindy, Willie, Archie, Amy, and Cody. They would live in the new house that Nick would help him build, and everything would be wonderful. Yes, that's what he wanted.

Lost in his own thoughts, he didn't realize he was in town, until Josiah had to repeat three times, "Brian! We're here!"

Brian blinked and pulled in the reins. "Oh, sorry."

Josiah and Nick climbed out of the wagon, and Brian followed. Josiah walked toward the hotel and then turned back. "Brian, you can't be dreaming. I know you just went through something really emotional, but you have to be aware of everything from now on. The town is in danger. You, Lindy, and Cody are in particular danger. As Jenna would say, 'you need to get it together, dude!'"

Brian nodded. "Yeah, all right. I need to go see Lindy and get the children. I'll talk to you later. See you, Nick."

Nick walked up to Brian. "I'm coming with you. I need to get prepared for my guard duty tonight."

They walked in silence to the house, and Nick opened the door for Brian to walk in. He saw the children playing on the floor of the living room. Rachel sat with them. "Rachel, where's Lindy?"

Brian's three children all said, "Hallo, Pa!"

"She's in her room, Brian. Just there, to your right." Rachel stood up and walked up to Nick. "What happened with Ray after you guys left? Sarah told me what happened here."

Brian didn't hear the rest of the conversation because he knocked on the door to Lindy's room. "Lindy? Open the door. I'd like to talk to you." He heard the sound of muffled crying coming from inside. "Please, Lindy. Let me hold you and make you feel safe." No response. "Lindy, I care about you. You're important to me. Please open the door and let me help." Although he felt self-conscious about saying these things in public, he also felt that Lindy needed to hear them, and that was more important. "Lindy, come on. Open the door." He put his hand on the handle and turned it, but then heard a voice behind him.

"I wouldn't do that, Brian. If she needs to be alone right now, leave her alone." Nick was shaking his head slowly.

"But I just want—"

"You have to do what *she* wants right now. And she wants to be left alone, so I think it's a good idea to do that."

Brian clenched his teeth and blinked his eyes. "You're right, Nick. It would make *me* feel better to comfort her." He sighed. "Thanks, man."

"Josiah is going to work out a schedule for guard duty. You can try the general store for a gun. And Josiah will tell you when it's your turn."

"I do have a rifle," said Brian without enthusiasm.

"That would probably be fine. I've got to run now." Nick kissed his two boys and Rachel good-bye and ran out the door, rifle in hand.

Brian shuffled into the living room. "Come on, children. Time to go home."

"Pa, the game is almost finished. Can we have a few more minutes?" asked Willie.

Brian opened his mouth to demand that they get up immediately and come with him, and then he changed his mind. He couldn't take out what he was feeling on the children. That wouldn't be right. "Yeah, all right."

Rachel stood up and put her hand on his arm. "Brian, if it's any consolation, I agree with Nick. You need to leave Lindy alone if that's what she needs. So there you have it from a woman's perspective."

"Thanks, Rachel. I appreciate that." He sat down on the arm of the sofa and watched the children play.

A few minutes later, Willie jumped up and down. "I won! I won!"

The children stood up and walked over to him. He stood up, too. "Bye, Rachel. Thanks for taking care of my children—and everything." Amy was so tired that she could barely stand, so he picked her up. Rachel let them out the door.

Brian walked up the street and put Amy into the back

of the wagon across her two brothers' laps. Then he climbed into the driver's seat and asked Dolly to move forward. It was dark, and he had only driven to the house a few times, but he trusted Dolly to know the way.

As he passed the turnoff to the cave, he thought about Nick sitting out there all on his own. And that made him think about Lindy, alone in her room, crying into a pillow, and not allowing him to comfort her. Why wouldn't she let him in? He knew she was upset about what happened, but he wanted to make her feel better. It made him feel bad that she wouldn't allow him to do that.

Dolly turned into the ranch, and Brian encouraged her closer to the house instead of stopping at the barn. He toted Amy into the house, and the two boys, just as tired, sleepily followed. After Brian got them all into bed and ready for sleep, he walked back outside with a flickering lantern from the house, and put Dolly into the barn with some fresh hay. Then he walked back to the house and got ready for bed.

Lying there in bed, looking out the window at the stars, he couldn't help but think that Lindy was under the same sky. Brian wished that she was right there with him. He wished that they were already married. Because he knew now, that is what he wanted—for them to be together always. Yes, her ex-husband coming to town was an obstacle, but not an insurmountable one. They'd work it all out. He'd make sure that she would feel safe again. He loved her.

CHAPTER THIRTY

LINDY HAD HEARD Brian talking to her through the door, but she wasn't going to invite him in. She had to leave the old Red Bluff, so there was no use in encouraging him. Although she cared about him, she wasn't staying. There was no choice about that. Her being here was putting everyone else's lives at risk. And she wasn't the kind of person who did what was best for herself without regard to the consequences to other people. What *was* best for herself, though? She thought she was safe here. If she wasn't safe here, would she be safe anywhere?

The conversation between Nick and Brian also bothered her. Guard duty? What was that about? Oh, she knew exactly what that was about. Guard duty against Ray. They had sent him home, but even they knew that he would return. It was another confirmation that leaving was the right thing to do.

Shortly after Brian and his children left, Cody came into the room. He climbed onto the bed and snuggled with her. "I didn't win, Mommy, but I had fun playing!"

"That's all that matters, sweetheart. Why don't you get into your pajamas now and come to bed?"

"Okay, Mommy. Can I turn on the lantern?"

"No, sweetie. You can get dressed in the dark. Your PJs are at the foot of the bed." She didn't want him to see the red streaks that she knew covered her face. The tears hadn't even dried yet. And her eyes would be so red. He couldn't miss that. If he asked why, it would be even worse, although when they left here, he'd have to know.

When Cody finished getting into his pajamas, he crawled into bed next to her. "G'night, Mommy." A minute later, she heard the soft, gentle sound of his breathing. He was already asleep. Lindy hoped that she could fall asleep that fast, so she wouldn't have to think anymore. She had already made her decision, now all she had to do was live with it.

The next morning when she awoke, she looked around the room and appreciated the rustic quality of it all. She felt happy that she was here in this safe place. Then she remembered. No, it wasn't safe. Not for her. Not anymore. Lindy blinked her eyes to keep from crying again. All she needed to do was to find someone who would transport her and Cody back to the twenty-first century. It shouldn't be that difficult.

After she got dressed, she packed all their belongings into the backpack and duffle bag that they had brought. All the clothes that Brian had bought her—except what she was wearing—were left on the end of the bed. Then she gently woke Cody and helped him get dressed. When they walked out from the bedroom, she saw that breakfast was on the table.

"I didn't want to disturb you, but I hoped that you would smell breakfast and feel hungry enough to eat." Rachel sat at the table with a cup of coffee. Another one was already poured.

"I'm starved! Where are the boys?" Lindy sat down and pulled out the chair for Cody.

"They've already eaten and are in the bedroom getting dressed for school." Rachel looked at Cody. "Are you ready to start school today, Cody?"

Lindy shook her head. "No, he's not going. We're leaving today," she said quietly.

"Mommy, I want to go to school with Oscar and Jamie! And Willie and Archie and *Amy*!" he said, pulling on her sleeve. "I like it here. I don't want to leave."

"We'll talk about it later, Cody."

"No! I don't want to leave!" He filled his mouth with two more bites of egg, slid off the chair, ran into the bedroom and slammed the door.

"What a mess. Rachel, I have to leave. You heard what happened last night. Ray found his way here somehow and threatened us with a gun. Brian stood between me and Ray! He risked his life for me!"

Rachel shrugged. "A man like that is hard to find, Lindy. If it were me, I wouldn't be so eager to leave him behind."

"I have to! I have to leave so everyone else will be safe. Ray is dangerous. It's better if he's just dangerous for me and not everyone else."

"What about Brian? What about everyone else who has gotten to know you and cares about you? What about them?

"I don't feel like I have a choice, Rachel. I have to go."

"Okay, listen. You don't have anyone lined up to take you back yet, right?" When Lindy nodded her head, Rachel continued. "Why don't you let Cody at least start school? Then, if no one can take you until tomorrow or something, at least he's taken care of."

Lindy moved her head from side to side and put her hand over her face. "Yeah, all right. I'm so confused right now, Rachel." Tears started sliding down her face, and she didn't stop them.

"Great, it's settled." Rachel took the plates off the table and put them on the counter. "Then you can go up to the hotel to see who is available to take you back."

CHAPTER THIRTY-ONE

BRIAN WOKE UP early, got the children ready, and drove the wagon into town. He was eager to see Lindy to make sure she was all right. As the children climbed into the wagon, Willie said, "Pa, why are you taking your rifle? Are you going hunting today? I can help!"

"No, Willie, I'm not going hunting. I just want to carry it with me today, that's all." He didn't normally lie to his children, he believed in telling them the truth. But this seemed like an extraordinary circumstance. How do you tell your children that someone wants to kill you?

Dolly trotted all the way to town, probably because she could feel Brian's excitement. When he pulled up in front of the livery, Ezra came right out and said, "I'll take care of it for you, Brian." Brian helped Amy down, and the four of them walked to the hotel. When they walked by the house where Lindy and Cody were staying, he hoped she would come out the door as he walked by, but that didn't happen.

They reached the hotel, and Brian held the door open so the children could walk in. Eliza was standing there, and they ran into her arms. "Gramma!" She hugged them all as Brian watched, and when she picked her head up, he saw there were tears in her eyes.

"What's wrong, Ma?" Brian asked, concerned.

"I never thought I'd have grandchildren." Then she broke away from the children and gave him a big hug.

"I love you, Ma, and I'm glad to be back." Their intimate moment was interrupted by Granny's raised voice in the kitchen.

"I don't care if you are sheriff, Josiah Stone, you can't tell me what to do. And I'll have you know that I was shooting from horseback—and winning—before you were born! Who do you think taught your wife, Jenna, to be such a good shot? Edward and I are doing it, and you can't stop us!"

When Brian and Eliza looked in, they saw Granny standing up to Josiah with her arms crossed. She looked half his size. "What's going on?" asked Brian.

"We need to have a meeting for everyone who will be standing guard, but then I didn't know who could guard the cave during the meeting. Granny volunteered, but I think it's too dangerous for her and Edward out there." Josiah looked down at Granny with his arms crossed like hers.

Granny waved her pointed finger at Josiah. "Dangerous schmangerous! You're just afraid that I'm a better shot than you! And another thing! I'm not asking that you include us for your regular guard duty! We just want to do it while you have the meeting! It's logical, Josiah Stone! Don't be a nincompoop!"

Eliza spoke up. "Josiah, she's right. If Granny says she's a good shot, I believe her. And I know my dad is a good shot. They'll be fine there during the meeting. Besides, I don't think that man will come back this soon, anyway."

"All right, Granny. You and Edward go. But take care of yourselves!" Josiah stood there with his hands on his hips.

"Woohoo!" Granny slapped herself on her hip, ran over to Edward, gave him a high five, and ran out of the room.

"Thanks, Josiah. You won't be sorry. My bride is a crack shot, and I'm pretty dang good myself!" said Edward, walking toward the door.

A minute later, Granny came down the stairs, toting two rifles and a gun belt. "Don't tell me that we're not prepared!" Edward buckled the gun belt around his waist, and they walked out of the hotel, each of them carrying a rifle. "We're taking the wagon, Brian!" drifted into the room right before the door closed.

"Hallo, Brian. I'm glad you're here," said Josiah. "We'll start our meeting as soon as Nick gets back. Why don't you go over to the general store to see if Ryan has a gun that would work for you?"

Brian nodded. A gun was the last thing in the world that he wanted, but for Lindy, he'd do anything. "I'll be right back." Then he saw the children with Eliza. "And you children behave while I'm gone. Listen to your Gramma."

"Brian," Eliza said, "they need to go to school today. Have they been to school before?"

"No. But I gave them their lessons every night. I don't think they'll have much catching up to do." He opened the door. "See you later, children. Have a good day at school!" They ran to him, and he kissed each of them on the top of the head.

"You know, Brian, Amy's awful young for school.

Perhaps she should stay here, and I'll just send the boys."

"Amy can already read, and we've been working on writing. I'm sure she'll be fine." Brian walked out the door and closed it behind him.

As soon as Brian walked into the general store, Ryan saw him and said, "Hey, Brian. Hear you're looking for a gun."

"Hi, Ryan. Yup. I don't want one, but I need one. Could you give me a loan until this incident is over?" Brian leaned over to pet the big dog at his feet.

"Sure. Not a new one, but I have several used ones that you're welcome to borrow." Ryan took away two of the guns that were displayed on the counter. "Any of these. And they're all tested and all accurate."

Brian walked up to the counter and looked at the guns. When he picked one up, bile immediately began to come into his mouth. He had to swallow it down quickly. He hadn't realized how distasteful he considered guns. Although he knew he didn't like them, his body's response surprised him. His time in the war taught him one thing: he wasn't the killing kind. Having to aim his gun and shoot at men and boys—with the intention of killing them—he didn't want to pick up a gun ever again.

But here he was, and he did it gladly for Lindy. One by one, he picked up all the guns on the table, feeling their weight and how they felt in his hand. "I'll take this one. Do you have a gun belt to go with it? And some ammunition?"

CHAPTER THIRTY-TWO

LINDY STOOD IN the doorway of the house as Cody held Rachel's hand to cross the street. Oscar held Jamie's hand, but when they got close to the other side, they ran the final five feet. Rachel didn't let go of Cody's hand until they had completely crossed, and then he ran off with the boys. Lindy smiled as she watched.

Cody liked it here. He felt comfortable here. Of course, he didn't know yet that his father had shown up. He probably wouldn't be comfortable after that. And there was nothing Lindy could do to keep that information from him. Someone would eventually tell him.

When Rachel and the kids entered the school, Lindy closed the door. The packed duffle and backpack were now on the bed waiting for her to find someone to take her back. She had no idea where to look or who to find. There weren't that many people in town who knew about the new Red Bluff, and even fewer who knew the way. Brian had been there, but after only one trip, he probably didn't know the way—not that she would ask him, anyway. She needed to stay away from him—that was better for both of them. No reason to get either of their hopes up when Lindy knew that she had to leave.

After taking one last look at her little room, she stepped out the door and headed toward the hotel. She'd start there. And besides, she wanted to explain to Eliza about why she couldn't work today. Although, she was sure that Eliza had heard the whole terrible story by now. When she came through the door of the hotel, she heard men's voices coming from the restaurant and saw Eliza standing in the doorway.

Eliza turned around when she heard the door close. "Lindy! Are you all right? I've been so worried about you!" She walked over to Lindy and wrapped her arms around her in a big hug.

Lindy, taken aback by the gesture, closed her eyes and enjoyed the moment. "Well, now you know why I can't work today. I need to leave."

"Leave? What do you mean, leave?"

"You know, go back *there*. So everybody here will be safe. I can't risk everybody's safety by staying. I'm not that kind of person." Lindy stepped back to look at Eliza.

Eliza smiled and slowly shook her head. "Lindy, we *want* you here. You're part of us now. You can't leave." She reached out and touched Lindy's shoulder. "You and Cody belong here. Besides, you probably haven't considered the whole situation. If you left, how would Ray know you were gone? He'd come back here looking for you, and if you weren't here, he'd figure we were hiding you. Lindy, the guy is a maniac. Leaving here isn't going to protect us from his insanity."

Before Lindy could recover from what Eliza had said —because it was all too true—how *would* Ray know, she heard Josiah's voice calling her from inside the restaurant.

"Lindy! Good that you're here. Please come in." After Lindy reluctantly walked in, Josiah said, "Lindy, I'm not sure if you know everybody here." Josiah started at the front and worked his way back. "This is Matthew, he owns the saloon—Sarah's husband; you know Ryan, I think; and Brian, of course." Lindy smiled shyly at Brian. "And you know Nick, since you're staying with him and his wife! Do you know Kat, Jenna's sister? And that's her husband, Doc; and in the back there is John Mills, president of the bank."

Lindy nodded to everyone. "Nice meeting all of you."

"We're all here to protect you. So you have absolutely nothing to worry about," said Josiah.

"She wanted to leave town to keep us all safe," called Eliza from the doorway.

"Oh, no. That would be the wrong thing to do, Lindy. He'd come back here wondering where you were, and no telling what havoc he would create if he couldn't find you. You need to let us protect you."

"Thank you," said Lindy.

"Lindy," said Nick, "the first thing that's going to happen is that I'm going *there* to report that Ray had a gun—which is illegal for a felon—and that should get his parole revoked. It shouldn't be a problem reporting it, because I'm a former officer of the law there. Once he's back in prison, you'll have nothing to worry about."

"Until then, we'll have a guard at the cave twenty-four hours a day," said Josiah.

"What about when he gets out of prison again? He knows where the cave is."

Josiah shook his head. "We'll deal with that if and when it comes up."

"Okay. Can I go now?" asked Lindy, uncomfortable standing there with everyone looking at her.

"Sure. We're talking about final logistics right now. Thanks. And remember, we'll keep you safe!" Josiah shook his fist in the air.

"Thank you." As she started to walk out, Brian took her hand as she passed. He smiled and winked at her. Somehow she managed to smile back, but she pulled her hand away and kept moving. Eliza was behind the front desk talking to someone, so she closed the door to the restaurant as she left. Strangers didn't need to know what was going on in there.

Walking out the front door, she didn't know where to go. Cody was at school and would be busy all day. She crossed the street and looked over the swinging doors into the saloon. No one was in there, but Sarah sat behind the piano belting out "Wind Beneath My Wings." That made Lindy smile, but she didn't want to disturb Sarah. So she walked slowly back to the house thinking over everything that had just happened.

They wanted her here! They really did. And they would protect her. What incredibly kind, wonderful, and generous people. They didn't even seem angry at her for disrupting their lives like this. If she was actually staying here, and it looked like she was, could there be a chance for her and Brian? Maybe, but she wasn't going to take any chances with his life. She had noticed the gun belt that he wore—so unlike him. No, she would not get involved with him until Ray was back in prison, and maybe not even then. She couldn't do that to anyone, but especially him. Because the truth was that she was falling in love with him. And although it would tear her apart to reject his attentions, she had to do that so she could keep him safe.

CHAPTER THIRTY-THREE

Brian sat on a rock near the mouth of the cave thinking about the past few minutes. When he approached the cave on a borrowed horse, he heard Granny say, "Who goes there? Show yourself or I'll shoot you down where you stand!" He came out of the brush and there she stood, rifle on her hip and her finger on the trigger. The gun was pointed right at him.

"But Granny," he had said, "you're supposed to be guarding the cave from people coming through it, not coming from town."

She had put the gun down and grinned. "I know. I was just funnin' with ya. I wanted you to know that I was ready for anything."

Edward put his arm around her. "Yep, this is my trigger-happy bride. Just don't make her mad, and everybody will get along fine."

Brian and Edward laughed, and Granny snickered. Brian climbed off his horse and watched as Granny and Edward climbed onto theirs. Granny needed no help. She climbed onto Dolly like she did it everyday. He liked her. She was one of a kind, and she was perfect for his grandfather.

His mind drifted to Lindy and how she had pulled away from him. He didn't know what to think about that. She had smiled at him, though. Maybe she was just nervous—she must have been, meeting all those new people and all the attention focused on her.

Although he could hardly wait to get back and see her, he knew that when he left his post at the cave, he would only have time to eat a quick supper and then drive the children home to Josiah's ranch. They were up late the previous night, and he didn't want to do that to them again. Children needed their sleep. So did he.

A rider approached, and when he walked out of the brush, it was Nick, whom Brian was expecting. "Hey, Brian. I'm on my way. And I'm hoping that this will take care of it, and we can all relax."

"Hallo, Nick. I was wondering—I know you have your hands full with going to the parole officer and all, but do you think you'll have any extra time?"

"Sure, Brian, what do you need? Ice cream? Cake?" Nick laughed.

"No, I was thinking of those little horses—ponies—any chance you could check them out for me?"

"Oh, sure! The parole office will be a quick visit. No problem. So you looking for three ponies for your kids?"

Brian nodded. "Well, yeah. And one for Cody as well."

"You are serious about that, then, aren't you?"

"I want to marry her, Nick. I really do."

"I'll see what I can come up with then. I may not be able to find four ponies today, though. I'll do my best, but I need to get moving now! See ya soon!" Nick waved as he disappeared into the cave.

Brian tried to make himself comfortable on the rock, but finally moved onto the ground and leaned against it for support. Then he picked up a stick and began drawing in the dirt. He wasn't much of an artist, so he was just passing time, drawing simple pictures. When he drew a picture of a house, it gave him an idea. Shifting around to make himself more comfortable, he began designing the house that Nick was going to help him build.

How many bedrooms should it have? Willie should have his own, Amy would need her own, and Cody and Archie could share one, and then a bigger one for him and Lindy. That would be perfect. Four bedrooms. And then he remembered a conversation that he had with Nick about the future. Nick had said that in the future, nearly every house had more than one bathroom— where the necessary was. With two adults and four children living in one house, two bathrooms sounded perfect, one for the children, and one for him and Lindy. That made sense to him. Hours passed as he drew the layout, rubbed his hand in the dirt to erase, and drew it again. Finally he had exactly what he wanted. He stared at the design to memorize it. It would be perfect!

When he heard a sound coming from the cave, he stood up, holding his rifle. He held his breath and didn't relax until he saw Nick. Behind Nick's horse were two ponies attached to each other with a rope. In his hand, Nick held a rope attached to the first pony.

"What do you think?" asked Nick.

"Oh, they're beautiful!"

"And they're very gentle, too. Perfect for your children. The other two are, also."

Brian looked behind him into the cave, but didn't see

any other ponies. "What other two?"

"Zack is bringing the other two. He should be just a few minutes behind me." Nick shook the rope to keep the lead pony from crowding.

"I owe you some money, Nick. Not only the ponies, but the supplies that we bought at the lumber store."

Nick nodded. "You still have plenty of money, Brian. Just let Zack know, and he'll give me what you owe me."

"That sounds good. I'll tell him."

Nick looked at him with a serious expression. "Listen, Brian, I have bad news about Ray."

"They didn't believe you?"

"No, it wasn't that. He believed me, all right. But Ray hasn't reported in. They already have a warrant out for his arrest."

"So they don't know where he is?" asked Brian.

"They have no idea. I'm sorry. There's nothing more we can do except keep up our vigil here."

"This is really bad. Lindy isn't going to take this well at all. I'd like to tell her myself."

"I knew you would. Listen, Zack isn't coming just to bring the ponies, he's going to rig something up in the tunnel so we can see around that corner—something with mirrors. It's a great idea, really. But I knew that you'd want to tell her, so I asked Zack if he wouldn't mind standing guard duty for a while."

"Oh, that's great! Thanks, Nick. I appreciate that."

"Zack should be here shortly. I'll get these ponies taken care of."

"Nick, wait. Can you see down here?" Brian pointed to the ground. "The layout of my new house."

"It looks big, Brian! But I guess you do have a big family. You know, though, that our building plans have to

144

wait for this Ray thing to end. Except for tonight, I'll be on night duty. But I can show you how to use the chain saw so you can cut down trees for the house and clear the way."

"Thanks, Nick. I already talked to the banker, when I met him this morning, and told him I wanted it. Tomorrow, I can go over there and do the paperwork. Thanks for everything!"

"Good luck with telling Lindy about this. I agree with you. She's not going to take it well." Nick turned around. "I hear something in there. It's probably Zack. I'll get going now. Bye."

Brian heard the sounds coming from the cave, so he picked up his rifle, just in case.

CHAPTER THIRTY-FOUR

LINDY POURED HERSELF another cup of coffee. Luckily the water still had a little heat to it. And that would have to do. She knew nothing about starting a fire or even getting it going again, and she didn't want to take a chance of doing something wrong. If she was going to stay here, and she hoped she was, she would have to get someone to teach her how to start a fire. The days of central heat or plugging in a small electric heater were long gone.

The idea of staying in the old Red Bluff gave her a certain thrill. She could feel it in her stomach traveling up to her shoulders. It was so cool here! Once she learned how to start a fire, she'd be fine. Using an outhouse would have been a drag, but since most of the "newcomers" had composting toilets now, well, she could deal with that. It had only been a few days, and she was already used to the one in Nick and Rachel's house.

And Cody not only fit in here, but he liked it here. He enjoyed playing with the other children. And he even had a girlfriend—Amy, Brian's youngest. How cute was that!

She sighed. It all sounded so easy and so peaceful. And thinking back on the conversation in the hotel, Nick was going to report Ray to the parole officer for having a gun. That would fix everything, wouldn't it? They'd find him, arrest him, and put him back in prison. Problem solved! Then she and Cody could get on with their lives here, and maybe, no, definitely, she could be with Brian then. Because with Ray in prison, she didn't need to stay away from him any longer.

With thoughts of Ray back in prison, Lindy finally allowed herself to relax. Kicking her feet out in front of her, crossing her legs at the ankles, she leaned back in the chair. For the first time since she heard Ray's voice while she was eating supper at Eliza's, she felt comfortable— not that walking-on-eggs feeling that she had almost every day of her marriage to Ray. Comfortable. And how great it felt. When she felt like this, she thought that she could allow Brian into her life. Why shouldn't she? She was in love with him, wasn't she? What was to stop her? Because if Ray was back in prison, like he would be soon after Nick reported the gun, then she could do what she wanted. And what she wanted was to be with Brian.

After taking a last sip of coffee, she allowed her mind to wander. Brian was building a new house—probably a log house. And she had always loved log houses. But that's not what Ray had wanted, so of course, she had to go along with him. Living with Brian and the children in a log house, how wonderful that thought was. Cody going to school in a one-room schoolhouse, and her keeping house for the family. She imagined herself in the kitchen washing the family's dishes—by hand, naturally —and looking out the window to a pasture full of cows. Although she was a city girl, the thought of looking at cows in a pasture sounded very serene. And she could use some serene in her life right now.

Sitting up in the chair, she began to feel so good that she decided to go tell Eliza that she would work the following day. She might as well. Since she was staying, she should work while she was here. Once she was in their own house—hers and Brian's—then she could keep house, but now, all she had was her little room. And she could help Rachel with the rest when she got off work. Although without a toilet to scrub and sinks to wash, there wasn't much to do.

She leaned forward putting her elbows on the table with her face resting in her hands, and she thought again about *their* house. How many bedrooms would it have? Let's see, Willie was the oldest, so he should have his own. Archie and Cody, being the same age, could share a room. Maybe bunk beds! Did they have bunk beds in the nineteenth century? And Amy, being the youngest and the only girl, would have her own room. And then she and Brian would have the master bedroom. It sounded so good that she didn't want to give up thinking about it to walk up the street to tell Eliza. Maybe just a little longer imagining the wonderful house that they'd live in.

And then she heard a knock at the door.

CHAPTER THIRTY-FIVE

WHEN BRIAN KNOCKED and Lindy opened the door, she had a smile on her face and so hopeful—and so beautiful. How he hated to destroy that look. And then, something overcame him. He opened his arms, pulled her to him, and kissed her. She kissed him back, but still, he felt uncomfortable with his impulsive action. "I'm sorry, Lindy. I'm sorry. Don't be mad."

Lindy smiled warmly. "I'm not mad. I kissed you back, didn't I?"

Brian, shyly, looked down and stuck his hands in his pockets. "Yeah, I guess you did."

"Do you want to come in?" She led him to the kitchen table and then sat down.

He sat across from her, reached out, and took her hands in his. Looking into her eyes, and with pain in his own heart having to tell her this, he said, "I have bad news, Lindy. Ray didn't report to the parole office. They have no idea where he is."

She pulled her hands from his and leaned back in her chair, looking to the side to avoid his eyes. Shaking her head, she said, "I should have known that Ray would

149

spoil things for me. He always does. Just when I was starting to feel good again." Exhaling sharply, she looked down and rubbed at her eye.

"Lindy, listen, I understand. But we're still out there guarding the gate until they find him."

"More likely, he'll find us first."

He reached for her hand, but she pulled it away. "Someone is guarding that cave night and day, and no one—including Ray—can get through."

"Brian, this whole thing makes me sick. And it's all my fault. I should have never come here."

"Lindy, do you really believe that?" He reached for her hand again, and she allowed him to hold it for a second, before slowly pulling away again.

"I don't know. I know that I hate this. I feel like I'm tied to him with a cord, and at the end of that cord is a bomb. And I have no idea when it's going to go off; I just know that it will."

"Lindy—"

"And I was about to go to the hotel to tell Eliza that I'd work tomorrow, but now—this." She put her face in her hands and began weeping.

Brian leaned forward, but didn't touch her. "Lindy, you *should* work tomorrow. It's better than sitting around here imagining the worst. Come on, let me tell my mother that you'll be in tomorrow."

She looked at him with a tear-stained face. "Do you really think that it will be better for me?"

Her receptivity gave him hope. "I do, Lindy, I really do. Will you let me tell her? Please?"

"Okay." After wiping away her tears, she pointed to his gun belt. "That doesn't look like it belongs to you."

Brian grimaced. "I borrowed it from Ryan at the

general store. I don't like guns."

"And it's because of me that you have to wear it!" Lindy's tears started streaming down her face again.

Without thinking, Brian leaned forward and hugged her to him. "Listen. I'm doing this because I want to. Yes, I don't like wearing a gun. But I do it gladly for you. I want you in my life. I want us to be a family. And if this is what I have to do to make that happen, I'm willing."

Lindy pulled away and said, "I want one, too."

"What?"

"One of those." She pointed at his gun.

"You want a gun? Why?"

"It will make me feel safer."

"Do you know how to shoot a gun?" Brian knew that Granny could shoot, Jenna could shoot, and apparently Jenna's sister, Kat, could shoot, because she was going to take six hours of guard duty the following day. So maybe all women in the twenty-first century could shoot. Still, he had to ask.

Lindy shrugged her shoulders. "No. Would you teach me?"

Brian nodded. "Yes, I'll teach you. But today, I have to get back to my post. I'm still on guard duty." He stood up to go.

Lindy's eyes got wide, and she had a sharp intake of breath. "You mean no one is there right now? He might have come through!"

Brian put his hand on her shoulders. "No, Lindy. Zack is there now. He said he'd watch so that I could come and tell you about Ray. I wanted to be the one to tell you."

Lindy took a deep breath and nodded. "Okay. Thank you for telling me. I'm glad it was you, too." She stood

151

up and put one hand on his arm. "But, Brian, we can only be friends—until this is over. I can't take the risk that Ray will do something to you if he knows that I like you. Just friends. So no more kisses, okay?"

Brian leaned forward and gave her a quick kiss on the lips. "All right. No more." He walked to the door, opened it, and turned around. "Bye, Lindy." And she smiled at him.

CHAPTER THIRTY-SIX

LINDY STOOD IN the doorway watching as Brian untied the horse in the front, mounted, and rode away. When he passed out of sight, she walked to her bedroom and flung herself on the bed. In a moment, she rose, walked into the living room, and flung herself on the couch. Again she got up, walked around the couch, into the kitchen, and sat down at the table. Still not satisfied, she began pacing from the kitchen to the living room and back. Over and over, while thoughts raced through her head.

What was she going to do? Brian had kissed her! And she had told him that she liked him—which wasn't entirely true, since she was in love with him—madly in love with him, actually. But it was still more than she would have liked to admit to him. But he had said that he wanted her in his life, that he wanted to be a family. How could she forget what he said and just be friends after that?

And Ray! He was out there, loose, no one knew where he was, and he could be anywhere. He could be planning to return at this very moment. And he was crazy! Who knew what he could be planning? That scared her so much—not just for herself and Cody, but for all the wonderful people that she had met here, and of course, especially for Brian.

She sank down into the couch hoping to do her thinking there. But soon she was nodding her head and then her whole body started following along, so she stood up and began walking again. Apparently, her body needed to keep moving right now.

Okay, she thought, let me be logical about this. Tomorrow, she would work again, which she hoped would take her mind off Ray. And maybe tomorrow Brian would have time to teach her to shoot. Although she didn't want to have anything to do with guns or shooting, if she had one and knew how to use it, she knew that it would make her feel safer.

As if she could ever completely feel safe with Ray on the loose. But if she had some control over her destiny— by having the gun—it would make her feel better. Her whole life with Ray was characterized by Ray taking all of her power away. She had been helpless and at his mercy for years. And Ray wasn't exactly merciful.

Brian was the complete opposite. Thoughts of him lightened her mood and made her smile. If there was one thing that characterized Brian, it would be kindness. And thoughtfulness. And consideration for others. And he was a good father. And he was handsome. And he wanted *her* in his life! How awesome was that!

Lindy laughed, put her arms straight out, and twirled around. He wanted *her*! Her moment of joy was interrupted when the front door opened, and Rachel and the three boys walked in. But she still had a smile on her face.

"Mommy!" Cody ran up to her and threw his arms around her.

Lindy swung him around. "Did you have a good day at school?"

"Yes! I had fun!" He leaned up to her ear and whispered, "Amy was there."

Lindy hugged him and said, "You were nice to her, weren't you?"

"I'll always be nice to her, Mommy. I like her."

"Cody, come on, let's play," said Jamie, who sat on the floor and began taking the pieces out for a board game.

Cody ran off, sat down next to Jamie, then stood up and ran back to Lindy. "I love you, Mommy!" And then he kissed her cheek and ran back to the game.

"How'd he do in school?" Lindy asked Rachel.

"He did great, and it looks like you did, too. You're certainly in a different frame of mind than when I left you this morning." Rachel sat down at the kitchen table.

Lindy sat in the chair opposite her. "Brian kissed me! And he told me that he wanted me in his life!"

"Wow! Things are progressing quickly."

"I really like him, Rachel." She looked down at her hands and then back up at Rachel. "That's not true. I'm in love with him."

Rachel blinked. "Wow!"

"I told him that we couldn't kiss anymore, and that we had to be just friends until this thing with Ray is resolved."

"What if it doesn't get resolved, Lindy? Nick stopped by today and told me that he didn't report in, so nobody knows where he is."

"I know. Brian told me." She looked down. "If it never got resolved, that would be horrible."

155

"There is a real chance that he has left the area and will never return. You could be doing all this worrying for nothing."

"I just hope he's caught soon."

"And if he's not, Lindy? What will you do, then?"

Lindy nodded her head. "Then I'll have to make a decision."

"I hope it's the right one for you and Brian," said Rachel.

Lindy slowly exhaled. "So do I," she said. "So do I."

CHAPTER THIRTY-SEVEN

BRIAN WOKE UP thinking about what a wonderful day it would be. Then he thought about how wonderful it had been to kiss Lindy the day before. And she had kissed him back! He could hardly wait to see her again. It was still too early to wake the children, so Brian lay in bed planning his day. But before he could begin, Amy came in and snuggled beside him. "Hi, Papa. I'm awake now."

"I see you are, sweetie. Would you like some breakfast?"

"All right. I'm hungry."

By the time he had started preparing breakfast, the two boys were up, so Brian fed everyone. An hour later, dressed and ready, they were on their way to town. In front of the hotel, he turned the wagon around, so it was facing the way they had just come. Brian and the children climbed out of the wagon and walked inside the hotel. "Ma! You here?"

Eliza hurried out from their living quarters, and the children surrounded her as if they hadn't seen her in ages, instead of just the previous day. "Well, what a delightful greeting!" She looked at Brian. "I dearly love having grandchildren, and I love that you're home with us again."

Brian didn't want her to start crying again, so he quickly said, "Remember, Lindy said she'd be in today. And I'm going to spend some time at my ranch right now."

"Ranch? You haven't bought the land yet, have you?"

Brian grinned. "That's what I'm going to do right now. Children, have a good day at school. Bye, Ma!" He kissed her on the cheek and rushed out the door, only to turn around and walk back in. "I forgot. Can I get some of that money, Ma?"

"Sure, Brian, I'll go get it." She returned a minute later with the sack of coins and handed it to him.

"Thanks, Ma. Is Jenna around?"

"Jenna? She and Josiah are in there." Eliza pointed into the restaurant.

Brian walked in and saw them sitting by the kitchen, their dogs at their feet. "Mind if I sit down?"

Josiah pulled out a chair. "Here ya go, Brian."

"Nothing happen last night?" Brian asked. Josiah had spent the night on guard duty at the cave. And although Brian didn't expect anything to happen, they were standing guard duty for a reason.

"All clear. I never heard a thing. Well, that's not true. I heard a sound of someone coming through the cave, I stepped back and pulled my gun, ready for anything. When the sound came closer, I turned on my flashlight and shined it into the cave, and out walks a four-point buck pretty as you please! He had already shed one antler, but the other one was still there. He was a beauty! Walked right on by me like I wasn't even there."

Brian leaned forward and whispered, "What's a flashlight? Is that a twenty-first-century gadget?"

Josiah and Jenna smiled at him. Milo, who was in Jenna's arms, gurgled. "You know the flickering lanterns at the house that look like real lanterns, but they have a switch to turn them on?" Brian nodded, so Josiah continued. "They're similar to that, but they have a bright straight beam ahead. Ask Nick to show you the one we have at the office."

Brian nodded. "All right." He looked at Jenna. "Jenna, I was wondering if you could do me a favor. Lindy wants me to teach her how to shoot, but I have no idea what kind of gun ladies would use. Any chance I could talk you into picking one out for her at Ryan's?"

"I can loan her mine—"

"No!" interrupted Josiah. "I want you to have that gun close to you."

Jenna looked at him surprised. "You *are* worried about this guy, aren't you?"

"I'd like to think that I scared him off and that he'll never come back, but that kind of arrogance gets people killed. Yes, I am worried. I think he's nuts and dangerous." He looked at Brian. "While I don't like the idea of Lindy having a gun if she doesn't know how to shoot one, I can't say anything, because there's a chance it could save her life."

"I'm going to teach her how to shoot today."

"Oh, much better, much better." Josiah stood up. "Well, I'm off to sleep now. It was a long night."

"Good-night, Josiah," said Brian.

Josiah leaned over and kissed Jenna and Milo. "G'night."

"Brian, I'll go over there right now to look at guns for you. Do you want me to ask Ryan to put it aside for

159

you?"

"Would you mind buying it for me, and I'll pay you back later? And bring it back here?"

"Sure, no problem, Brian. I think you're good for it!" She smiled at him. "I'll go over there as soon as I feed Milo."

Brian stood up abruptly. "Oh! All right! I'll see you later, Jenna! Thank you!" He walked out of the restaurant and didn't see anyone in the entryway, so he opened the front door and walked out. Heading up the street toward the bank, he wondered if Nick was up yet. Brian was supposed to meet him at the sheriff's office, but he couldn't tell if Nick was there or not.

He walked into the bank and walked up to the teller. "Is John Mills here?"

"I'm right in here, Brian, come in!"

The teller pointed the way to John's office, and Brian walked in there. "Hallo, John!" Brian shook his hand.

"Good to see you again, Brian! You've come about the property?"

Brian nodded and held up the bag of coins. "Yes, I have the money here."

"Great. It's one hundred sixty acres. Does that suit you?"

"Sounds perfect."

"There is a small cabin and an overgrown garden at the western edge of the property, but it wouldn't be difficult to remove if that's what you wanted to do. The previous owner decided frontier life wasn't for him and moved back to the city."

"I'll take a look at it, but that's fine. Where do I sign? Oh! And how much is it?"

"Two hundred dollars for one hundred sixty acres."

Brian plunged his hand into the coin bag and began pulling out coins and counting them out on the desk. When he reached two hundred, he put the last coin down and signed the paperwork.

John Mills stood up and shook Brian's hand again. "Congratulations," he said. "You're now a land owner. When I finish the paperwork, I'll bring it over to the hotel for you."

Brian nodded and smiled. "Thank you!"

As he walked out of the bank, Nick and Jenna were outside talking. "Hallo, Nick," Brian said.

"Hey, Brian. You ready to go?"

"Yeah." Looking at Jenna, he said, "Jenna, would you mind bringing this back to the hotel for me? You can pay for the gun from it, too." Jenna took the bag and raised her eyebrows at him. Understanding what she meant, he said, "Oh! If I can't trust the sheriff's wife, who can I trust?" Then the three of them laughed, and Jenna walked across the street toward the general store carrying the bag.

"Brian, can you pull the wagon around back so I can load the chain saw and the gasoline without anyone seeing?" asked Nick. "I'll meet you back there."

"I'll do it right now!" Brian smiled and thought about how wonderfully his life was coming together. He now owned his own land, he was about to start building his house, and his courtship with Lindy was progressing. Although he had agreed not to kiss her for a while, at least they'd be spending time together.

CHAPTER THIRTY-EIGHT

WHEN LINDY WATCHED as Rachel and the three boys walked across the street toward the school, she smiled. Cody was so happy to go to school here. In the twenty-first century, it was a fight every morning. Once he got there, he usually enjoyed it, but he never wanted to go. Here, he could hardly wait to go. Of course, his little girlfriend, Amy, was part of the reason that he loved school so much. Lindy chuckled to herself. They were so cute together.

She finished getting ready, stepped out the front door, inhaled deeply, and looked at the blue sky above her. Was it bluer here than in the new Red Bluff? It sure looked like it. That would make sense. Even the new Red Bluff, although it was just a small city, had some pollution that would affect the air quality and the air clarity. Shaking her head, she thought about how wonderful it was to live here, and how much she loved it. And she would love it even if Brian McKenna wasn't here! But she definitely loved it more with him in the picture.

Instead of crossing the street, she stayed on her side of the street and walked past the doctor's house and up to the saloon. She peered over the swinging doors to see if Sarah was at the piano again. Sarah and her husband were behind the bar, kissing. Lindy smiled and crossed the street. They made such a cute couple. Life here was so idyllic. Except for Ray—but she wasn't going to let thoughts of him interfere with her life here. The cave was guarded all the time, and she had to trust either that he wouldn't return, or that they'd catch him when he did. Or, ideally, that some law enforcement official would catch him in the twenty-first century.

Lindy entered the hotel with a smile on her face, and when she saw Eliza behind the counter, she walked right up to her and hugged her. "Hi, Eliza!"

"Well, hallo, Lindy. What's this about?"

"I want you to know how much I appreciate your kindness."

"My pleasure. You ready to work today?"

"Sure am! That's why I'm here. I thought Brian would have told you."

Eliza shrugged. "He did tell me. I was just checking. I'm glad you're here now, because I could really use the help. Would you mind starting in the kitchen and doing the dishes?"

"Not at all. Thanks, Eliza." She kissed the older woman on the cheek and walked into the kitchen.

Before Lindy finished the dishes, some people came into the restaurant, so Lindy took their order and brought them coffee. Eliza started to cook their breakfasts, but was called to the front desk, so Lindy finished, and then served them. When the people left, and she had finished, Eliza called her to the front desk. Hours passed, and Lindy didn't even realize it.

"You can have some break time now," said Eliza.

"Already?" asked Lindy, surprised.

"You've been here since early morning, girl! You deserve a break! Jenna is in the restaurant, why don't you go talk to her?"

Lindy walked into the restaurant and saw Jenna. "Mind if I sit down, Jenna?"

"No, not at all. In fact, I wanted to talk to you." Milo was over Jenna's shoulder, and Jenna was patting him on the back.

"Oh? What about?"

With one hand, Jenna stuck her hand inside her shoulder bag, pulled out a gun, looked at it, said, "Oh, not that one," put it back, fished around again, pulled out a different gun, and put it on the table.

Lindy looked at it. "Okay."

"It's yours." Jenna pushed the gun toward Lindy. "Brian asked me to pick one out for you. Is this one okay?"

Lindy picked up the gun and held it in her hand. She shook it, looked at Jenna, and smiled. "I don't know anything about guns. I guess it's all right." Grimacing, and holding the gun away from her, she said, "Is it loaded?"

"Oh! Yeah, the ammunition." She fished inside her bag again and brought out a small box of bullets. "I mean, no, it isn't loaded. Here are the bullets." She pushed them over to Lindy. "Better put that in your purse. It's strictly twenty-first-century."

"Bullets?"

"No, not the bullets, the cardboard box. Just put it in your purse."

Lindy opened her own shoulder bag and stuffed the bullets in. But the purse wasn't as big as Jenna's, so it was a tight fit.

"I have an older, bigger shoulder bag that I gave to Ryan to sell. If it's still over there, you can tell Ryan that I said you could have it."

"Okay, thank you. I appreciate that." Lindy put the gun on the table. "I'm not sure I'm ready for this."

"When Brian told him, Josiah thought it was a good idea. That's why I'm carrying this." Jenna patted her shoulder bag where her own gun was. "Here, let me show you a couple of things before Brian gets here. He's coming today to show you how to shoot, right?"

"He said he would."

"Would you mind me showing you?"

"No, go ahead." Lindy pushed the gun toward Jenna, who picked it up.

Jenna shifted Milo over; he'd fallen asleep on her shoulder. "First, never ever ever point the gun at anybody or anything unless you intend to use it. Don't playfully point it at someone thinking that it's not loaded. A lot of people have died that way."

Lindy nodded. "Okay."

"And this is how you can check to see if it's loaded or not. Press your thumb right there and pop that thing out. Then hold it up and look through, and you can look into the chamber, too." Jenna moved the gun in front of Lindy so she could see.

"Yeah, there's nothing in there. I can see that!"

Jenna snapped the chamber shut and put the gun on the table. "That's the basics—except how to clean it. Brian can show you that and everything else."

Lindy picked up the gun and held it to her chest. "I think this is going to make me feel safe. At least, I hope it will."

CHAPTER THIRTY-NINE

IT WAS STILL early when Brian and Nick reached the new land. They pulled the wagon into the property, unhooked Dolly from the harness, and let her graze in the tall grass while they walked some of the property.

"Do you want to ride the whole property first to see where you want the house?" Nick looked across the great swath of land.

"No, I think I like it right up here on that little hill." Brian pointed to a hill south of where they stood. "It's close enough to the road for ease, yet far enough to be safe for the children to play. Yeah, right up there."

"All right, I'll carry the chain saw—I already filled it with fuel—and we can leave the gasoline here until we need it."

When they reached the top of the small hill, Nick placed the chain saw on the ground. "It's important to put the chain saw on a flat surface before you start it. Okay, first press this all the way down. Put your left hand on that bar and your right foot against that. Now pull the handle, and voilà!" Nick pulled the handle, the chain saw came to life, and Brian stepped back so quickly that he

166

fell down on his butt. They both laughed; Nick turned the chain saw off and gave Brian a hand to help him get up. "Come on. Now you try it."

After a couple of failed attempts, Brian got the chain saw roaring. He had a big smile on his face with his success.

Nick motioned to him to turn it off, so Brian flicked the switch. "It would be a good idea if you checked the road to make sure no one is coming. Josiah knows about this, but he isn't happy about it. On the other hand, he couldn't expect you to cut all these trees down by hand with this available. If someone does come along, try to hide it and make something up!"

Brian put the chain saw behind his back and put the other hand out palm up and said, "I was just trying out my lion roar voice!"

"Yeah, that will work!" said Nick, raising his eyebrows and shaking his head. They both laughed again. "Now let me show you how easy it is to cut down a tree. After a few minutes of instruction and some test tries, Brian figured it out and started cutting down trees. "Here," said Nick, stepping forward, "let me do a few. These over here?"

When they finished clearing the area where Brian wanted his house, they sat down on a tree close to the wagon. "I've had enough, Brian. You'll need more trees for your house, but if you want to do any more today, I think it's up to you! I still have to stand watch tonight." Nick wiped the sweat off his brow. "I need a shower!"

Brian looked at him confused and then nodded. "Are you talking about that water thing that Zack showed me in the house?"

"Yep, that's it. It is *very* refreshing when you're hot and

167

sweaty. I've thought of trying to rig one up here, but Josiah wouldn't hear of it in town like that. But out here —" Nick trailed off nodding his head. "Yeah, out here you could probably get away with it—even with Josiah across the street!"

"Maybe you can help me with that, too, after I finish the house."

"Dude, with all those rooms that you've planned for the house, I think that's going to be a long while!"

Brian laughed. "Yeah, but I have a big family. I need it."

"You ready to go back and drop me off?" Nick stood up and looked at Brian.

"Sure thing. You want to work on the rooms above the jail now?"

"No, I've had enough for one day. With me on guard duty every other night, this much work during the day is about all I have in me. I'll probably take a nap before I start this evening."

Brian hitched Dolly up to the wagon, the two men climbed in, and Brian asked Dolly to move. He glanced across the road to where Josiah and Jenna's house was and thought that it couldn't be a bad thing to have the sheriff living so close.

"So, will you work out there more today?" asked Nick.

"No, I'm going to the hotel to see if Lindy can get off for a while. I'm going to teach her to shoot. She said she'd feel safer that way."

"I don't blame her. That ex-husband of hers is a dangerous guy."

Brian drove the wagon through town, turned it around, and parked in front of the hotel. "Last stop, Red Bluff!" he pretended to announce.

"See ya later, Brian. Good luck on the shooting lessons!" Nick walked across the street to the sheriff's office.

When Brian walked into the hotel restaurant, he saw Lindy sitting with Jenna and baby Milo. The baby was sleeping across Jenna's shoulder, and Lindy held a gun to her chest like it was something that she treasured. Good, he thought. He smiled at the image. It was more difficult to teach someone to shoot if they were afraid of the gun. It didn't look like Lindy was.

"Hallo, ladies. You have time for some lessons today, Lindy?"

CHAPTER FORTY

LINDY LOOKED UP, pleased at the sound of Brian's voice. Before she could answer, though, Eliza strode into the room. "Yes, she has plenty of time, and if you'll wait a few minutes, I'll make a quick lunch that you can take with you!"

"Thanks, Ma!" Brian walked over and sat at the table next to Lindy.

"Thanks, Eliza. Can I help you with that?" Lindy stood up.

"No!" said Eliza from the kitchen. "You stay put. It's your break! I can take care of this."

Several minutes later, Brian and Lindy walked to the door. "Bye, Ma. Bye, Jenna!" called Brian.

"Thank you, Eliza! Thanks, Jenna!" called Lindy, as Brian swept her out the door. After Brian helped her into the wagon, he climbed in next to her and asked the horse to move forward. "Is this your horse? It's pretty."

"This is Dolly. She is the horse that Granny rides, but technically she's Jenna's horse. If you want to use her, though, you'll have to ask Granny!"

Lindy shook her head. "I don't really ride."

"But I saw you that first day that you came to town."

"Oh, I was riding behind Zack, but just to get here. And we were riding bareback! Did you see that?"

Brian nodded. "I did. Would you like to learn to ride? I can teach you that just like I can teach you to shoot!"

Lindy laughed. "One thing at a time, Brian!"

Brian held the reins with one hand and reached down with the other to gently take Lindy's. She looked down as if it wasn't her hand, but when he squeezed it, she smiled at him. "Where are you taking me, Brian?"

"To my place."

"You mean Josiah and Jenna's?"

"No, mine."

"You have your own place, already?"

"Yep. I bought it today!"

Lindy saw a ranch house on the left, with a big barn and a corral. So it confused her when he guided the wagon to the right. She looked at him and shrugged.

Brian stopped the wagon and smiled at her. "This is my place. Come look." He jumped out of the wagon, ran to the other side, and instead of helping her down, he picked her up and put her on the ground. "Come on." He took her hand and led her up a small hill where many trees had been cut down.

He made a sweeping motion with his hands. "This is what Nick and I did this morning." They walked into the middle of the fallen logs, and Brian pointed as he spoke. "Right here is the kitchen. And the living room and dining room will be here. This room will be Amy's bedroom, this will be Willie's, and this one over here will be for Archie"—he looked at her—"and Cody. Here is the bathroom for the children. And this big room over here will be for me—and you." He knelt down on one knee,

171

kissed her hand, and looked up at her. "Lindy, I want you to live here with me and be my wife. Please say yes."

Lindy felt shocked. She looked at him kneeling there, holding her hand, and she brought her other hand up to her mouth and blinked. Although he had talked about them being a family, she hadn't expected him to ask her to marry him this soon. But she *did* know that she was in love with him and wanted to marry him, so she smiled. He was looking up at her so expectantly. She removed her hand from her mouth and put it on the side of his face. "Yes, Brian, I'll marry you. But not"—she looked at him seriously—"until the deal with Ray is settled."

Brian stood up, still holding her hand in his. "I know I agreed to just be friends, but can I kiss my fiancée?"

Lindy threw her free arm around him, and Brian leaned down and kissed her. Then pulled away, looked at her, and said, "I love you so much, Lindy."

"I love you, too, Brian."

Then he pulled her to him and kissed her again. Lindy thought that it was the best kiss that she had ever had in her life. She pulled away from him. "Remember, no marriage until the issue with Ray is resolved."

Brian smiled and shrugged. "But I can start planning it, right? Tell Ma and all?"

Lindy looked at the ground and thought for a moment. "No, I don't think you should, Brian. If somehow he found out, *he* could kill both of us. He could hurt the children. I don't think it's a good idea."

Brian frowned. "You're probably right, although I don't think it's a problem now. Ray hasn't come back yet —didn't you figure that he'd return right away? I did. But he hasn't. I think we're safe now. He knows that he shouldn't stay in town, because they're looking for him. I bet he's long gone by now."

"Just to be safe, Brian? Please?"

He nodded and hugged her. "Okay, but *I* know. *You're* going to be *my* wife, and I couldn't be happier about it!"

CHAPTER FORTY-ONE

BRIAN LOOKED AT Lindy and saw love and hope on her face. He wanted to kiss her again, but he knew that they should do what they came there to do. "All right, let's get started. You ready?"

"I guess so."

Turning his head and frowning, he said, "Are you sure you want to learn this?"

Lindy exhaled. "I wish I didn't *have* to learn it, but yes, I'm ready."

When he started by showing her how to tell if a gun is loaded, she said, "I already know that!" and took the gun out of his hand to show him.

"Very good! I'm impressed. All right, here's how to load it, then." After showing her that, he showed her how to hold and aim the gun. When she fired the gun for the first time, she was surprised how much it sent her backwards. "That's why you have to aim carefully the first time," explained Brian. "You might not get a second shot. Aim for his heart."

Lindy, who had been shooting and reloading, and even hitting what she shot at, lowered her arm so the gun was

174

pointed toward the ground. "I don't want to *kill* him. I want to stop him from hurting us."

"Oh," said Brian, nodding his head. "You want *him* to kill you, then?"

"No," said Lindy, quickly shaking her head. "I want him to leave us alone."

"And you think that after you wound him, he'll do that?" Without waiting for an answer, Brian continued. "If you hit him in the arm, he will be so mad that he will rip you apart. And probably Cody, too, if he's close enough."

Lindy put her head down and nodded. "Yeah, you're right. That sounds like him." Picking the gun back up, she reloaded and started shooting again.

"There's a squirrel." Brian pointed to a squirrel in a tree. "Do you want to try to hit it?"

Lindy shook her head vehemently. "No! I don't want to hurt an animal!"

Brian put his arm around her and squeezed her. "I was hoping that you'd say that. I don't like to kill animals, either. Whenever I hunt, after I bring a deer down, I always apologize to it and thank it for feeding my family."

She looked up at him. "I love you so much, Brian. But I think we better get back now. I still have to work!"

He leaned down and kissed her. "I love you, too, Lindy. Let's get you back to work!"

On the way back to the hotel, he held her hand, and they talked about the new house. Lindy was as excited about it as he was, which made him feel good. Brian wanted to tell her about the little horses that he had bought for all the children, but since she wasn't ready to learn to ride yet, she probably didn't want Cody to learn

175

to ride, either, so he decided to wait. The conversation with Lindy was so pleasant, that they were at the hotel in no time, and Brian felt like he had barely spent any time with her.

"See you tomorrow for another lesson?" asked Brian, as Lindy stepped off the wagon.

"Same time, same station!" Lindy smiled up at him.

"What?" asked Brian, confused.

"Oh, sorry. Yup, tomorrow! See you then!"

Brian watched as she walked up to the door, opened it, and turned around and waved to him before stepping inside. He exhaled a deep, satisfied breath, closed his eyes, and thought about how grateful he was for the way everything was turning out.

Since the children weren't out of school yet, and he didn't want to drive back to the house again, he shook the reins and had Dolly turn two corners until he was at the back of the sheriff's office. Then he thought better of it and drove the wagon down in front of the livery. Ezra came out immediately and stood by Dolly's side.

"You done for the day, Brian, or will you be taking her home again?"

"I'll be taking her home in a couple of hours. But I do need another bale of hay."

"Sure thing. I'll have it loaded in the wagon by the time you return." Ezra waited until Brian got out of the wagon, and then he unhitched Dolly.

"Thanks, Ezra!" Brian decided to walk around to the front of the sheriff's office in case Nick was still sleeping. When he got there, Josiah was sitting at the desk. "Nick still sleeping?"

"I thought I heard him get up a few minutes ago. Listen, would you mind staying here until he gets out?

I'm sure he'll be quick. Tell him that I'll be back before he has to go to the cave."

"Sure, Josiah. I'll tell him."

"Thanks!" Josiah walked out the door, leaving Brian in the office alone.

That wasn't all he was going to tell Nick, he thought. He was brimming over just needing to tell someone about him and Lindy. Brian had told her that he wouldn't tell Ma, but there was no way he could keep this a secret. He had to tell someone!

When Nick came out of the bedroom in the back, he nodded, yawned, and rubbed his eyes. "Hey, Brian."

"Nick! Sit down! I need to tell you something, but you have to keep it an absolute secret—even from Rachel!"

CHAPTER FORTY-TWO

BACK AT RACHEL and Nick's house after spending part of the afternoon with Brian and part of the afternoon working at the hotel, Lindy stood beside Rachel helping her clean up after supper. Rachel had placed a special order with Ryan, so they had pizza for supper! And it was great! Ryan had kept two of them in his solar freezer until Rachel picked them up earlier in the afternoon.

"That was so great, Rachel. Thank you again for letting me stay here. I know it's an inconvenience—especially for the boys."

"No, it's not!" called Oscar from the living room, where the three boys were playing another board game. "We like having you here!"

"I love having Cody here!" yelled Jamie.

"See? There ya go." Rachel handed her another plate to dry. "It's unanimous. You're very welcome here."

"Okay, maybe, but I still feel guilty about Nick having to spend every other night with guard duty—directly because of me."

"He's the deputy sheriff. It's part of the deal. He doesn't mind, honestly. In fact, a little adrenalin will do him good. Sometimes he says this town is too quiet."

"Would he want to move back to the new Red Bluff?"

Rachel shook her head. "Definitely not. Both of us realize that in living here, we are giving up some modern conveniences and other lifestyle issues that we were used to in the new Red Bluff. But the advantages here so much more than make up for it!"

Lindy nodded. The secret knowledge that she was keeping inside her was busting to get out, and she didn't think she could hold out any longer. She glanced back to make sure the kids were engaged in the board game. "Rachel," she whispered, "I have to tell you something that is so secret, I have to ask you not to tell anyone, not even Nick." She looked at Rachel hopefully and raised her eyebrows.

"I promise on my honor as a woman!" Rachel placed her wet hand over her heart, making a water mark on her blouse. "Oops!" Both women laughed.

Lindy leaned over and whispered in Rachel's ear. "Brian asked me to marry him, and I said yes!"

Rachel let out a "whoop" and almost dropped the dish she was holding. Then she looked at Rachel and nodded. "Good work, girlfriend!"

"Please don't tell anyone. I wouldn't even let Brian tell Eliza."

"I promised, Lindy. I swear I won't tell a soul." She went back to the dishes. "So when's the big date?"

"I told him we couldn't do it until the thing with Ray is settled."

"Lindy, that could be a long, long time. Is it fair to make him wait that long?" Rachel handed Lindy another plate to dry. "And what if it doesn't get settled? Then, what?"

"I have to hope that it gets settled soon. Brian is building us a house!"

"I know. Nick is helping him."

"Oh, that's right. Nick showed him how to use the chain saw. Brian told me that." She dried the plate and put it in the cupboard. "His house—I mean our house—is going to have two bathrooms! One for the kids and one for us!"

"Sounds awesome."

Then Lindy sighed, disappointed. "But as big as the house is, it will take a while to build."

"It doesn't matter if they haven't caught Ray yet, right?"

Lindy nodded. "Yeah, you're right. I know it's a big restriction to put on Brian and the wedding, but I don't feel right doing it any other way. Ray is really dangerous, you know? He almost seems worse since he got out of prison. He never had a gun before—"

"Oh. I didn't know that. I don't think Josiah or Nick did, either."

Lindy looked down. "It's scary."

"Yeah, I think it is. It means he's stepped it up a notch. That's not good."

"See? That's exactly why I can't marry Brian until things get settled. It's not fair to him—and his children. Ray has already threatened to take Cody back with him —not because he wants him—but because he knows it would bother me. So if Brian and I were already married, then he could just as easily do that with Brian's kids." She shook her head. "I can't risk it."

"When you say it that way, it does make sense. On the other hand, you could wait forever. Ray may never get caught."

"Yeah, I have to admit, that is something to think about," agreed Lindy.

"Maybe you could leave the decision about the risk up to Brian. Let him decide. Explain it to him like you did to me. Then taking the risk is up to him."

"It just may come to that," said Lindy. "It just may come to that."

CHAPTER FORTY-THREE

RAY FELT SO excited he could hardly stand it. His hands were sweating, his heart was racing, and he could feel the adrenalin coursing through him. He knew what he wanted to do. Tonight, he would find out if it was possible. But he had a feeling it was, and he had a feeling that everything was going to work out exactly how he wanted it to.

After starting the motorbike, he turned it onto the trail. Although he wanted to crank it up all the way and go as fast as it would carry him, he maintained a slow speed. The turnoff was camouflaged enough that he might miss it in the dark. So he kept the bike going slow, and when he thought he was close, he would turn on the flashlight and shine it to the right. He hoped he could find it that way. Since he was now officially "on the run," his only choice was to come out here at night. But he could still find out what he needed to. It didn't have to be light to see that.

As he drove slowly through the night, he thought about the town where Lindy lived—the town with the sign that said *Red Bluff*. No matter how many times he went over it in his head, he couldn't figure it out. It looked like a movie set, but it obviously wasn't. What kind of a town in the twenty-first century has a sheriff that wears a gun on his hip? It didn't make sense. But it didn't matter. He would take care of them. All of them. And especially that guy she was having dinner with. Yeah, especially him.

Thinking of the sheriff's gun, he reached back and felt the gun in his back waistband. The sheriff had kept his other gun, but it was easy enough to get another. With his new connections that he had met in prison, he could get anything he wanted, anytime—like what he needed to complete this job. Lindy didn't realize what an incredibly great favor she had done by sending him to prison. Everything he learned there, the people that he met—it was better than a college education!

He flicked on the flashlight and pointed it to the right, and then his thoughts returned to Lindy. If there was a way to catch her on one side and the boy on the other, that would be best, but regardless, his plan was bound to work. Checking it tonight was a smart precaution to make sure it would go smoothly. And Ray liked to be smart. He may be mean, but at least he was smart. The thought made him laugh to himself. It made him laugh so hard that he almost missed the turn.

There was no reason, at this late hour, to hide the motorbike. Nobody else would be on this trail at midnight. So, he turned it off and put the kickstand down. Then he used the flashlight to avoid the rocks and brush as he trudged up the hill. When he got to the cave, he walked inside and without having to go too far, he found what he was looking for: a narrow ledge that was a few feet off the ground on the left-hand side, before the bend in the cave and almost directly under the narrow opening above. The ledge wasn't necessary, but Ray thought it would be better. And there it was, exactly as he hoped it would be.

He didn't walk through to the other side, because there was no need to. Quick in, quick out, and leave. That way, no one would know he had been here, and they wouldn't suspect a thing—exactly how he wanted it. No one saw him; no one heard him. It was his little secret. And for them—a big surprise. A *really* big surprise! He didn't know if there was an alternate way to get to the strange little town, but he hoped not. That would fix them.

Carefully, he walked back down the hill. All he needed now was to fall in the dark and get hurt. That wouldn't turn out good. So he slowly stepped over the rocks and avoided the bushes and soon was back down on the trail where the motorbike was.

He exhaled slowly, smiled, started the bike, climbed on, and headed back, this time not so slow. The trail back out to the street was wide and easily seen with the headlight. So he cranked it and sped off into the night, smiling as he went.

CHAPTER FORTY-FOUR

WHEN BRIAN AND the children bounded into the hotel the following morning, he noticed that his mother looked especially serious. He hugged her and asked, "What's the matter, Ma?"

"Nick came in this morning, frowning. He said to send you right in as soon as you arrived. Josiah's in there with him now." She gathered up the children who were about to run into the restaurant. "Come on, children, let's go in here today." And she led them into her sitting room.

Brian, concerned, walked into the restaurant and saw Nick and Josiah talking quietly at a table in the corner. When Josiah saw him, he waved him over.

"Brian, come on. You need to hear this," said Josiah. "Nick, start from the beginning again."

"Last night, around midnight, I heard what I thought was a motorcycle engine. But, you know, listening from the other side of the cave, it might have been an airplane. I ignored it until I heard something enter the cave. I wanted to believe that it was the deer that Josiah saw, but then in the mirrors, I saw a reflection of a flashlight." Nick reached across the table and patted Brian's hand. "I'm sorry, man. It had to be Ray."

"Go on, Nick," said Josiah.

"He didn't come all the way through the cave, just spent a few minutes on the other side of the bend. Then a few minutes later, I heard the motorcycle again. At first light, I walked through the cave to the other side, and besides some nondescript footprints in the dirt leading into the cave, I saw nothing. I have no idea what he was doing there. It was like he was checking something.

"He didn't see me, because Zack made sure to place the mirrors so they only worked from our side of the cave, and I didn't make a sound." Nick shook his head. "I can't figure it out. Either of you have any ideas?"

"I don't. It sounds curious, but I have no idea what it could mean," said Josiah.

Brian put his head in his hands. "Oh, man. When Lindy finds out about this——"

"When Lindy finds out about what?" asked Lindy, standing behind Brian, with her hands on his shoulders.

Brian shook his head, so Josiah cleared his throat and said, "Lindy, we strongly believe that Ray came to the cave last night. He didn't come all the way through it, just stayed on the twenty-first-century side and was there only a few minutes, but we're pretty sure that it was him."

Brian turned around and saw that Lindy had faltered behind him. Before he could stand up to catch her, Josiah was on his feet holding her up. Brian put his arm around her, and she pushed him away.

"No! Don't touch me! Don't talk to me! Just leave me alone! And it's off! It's completely off!" Then she stalked out of the room.

"What's off?" asked Josiah.

"I wasn't supposed to tell anyone, but I guess now it doesn't matter," said Brian. "Lindy and I were going to get married. I asked her yesterday, and she said yes, but we'd wait until everything got settled with Ray." He sighed and sank back into the chair. "And now this. I don't know what to do."

"We can go to town and catch him!" said Nick.

"Nick, you're not an officer of the law there, anymore. And I never have been. If something happened and Ray got shot, it would be you and me going to jail, not him. No. Impossible." Josiah sat down, shaking his head.

"What can we do then?" asked Brian.

"Wait until he comes back and get him then." Josiah shrugged. "There's nothing else we can do."

Brian stood up. "I'm going to go talk some sense into Lindy. We shouldn't let what *he* does affect what *we* want to do. If we do, then he wins."

He walked out of the restaurant and into the entryway, where his mother was behind the front desk. "Where's Lindy?"

"In there." Eliza motioned over her shoulder to her sitting room and dining room.

When Brian started walking in there, Eliza stopped him. "Brian! Stop!"

"Why? I need to talk to her."

"Not now, Brian. Lindy doesn't need to be talked to. She needs some time alone. She wanted to go home and not work today, but I promised her that I wouldn't let you near her. That was the only way she would consent to stay. So you need to go back in there and talk to your friends or go to your new place and work on that. What you can't do, is go in there and talk to her. Understood?"

Brian shook his head and blinked back the tears. "I

can't believe this is happening. I just can't believe it."

CHAPTER FORTY-FIVE

LINDY, SITTING AT the dining room table and gazing out the window, had heard what Eliza said to Brian, so she didn't think he would bother her now. At least not where she was sitting. She heard him walk away, but instead of the footsteps fading away into the restaurant, she heard the front door open. When he passed in front of the window and looked in, she looked away. He didn't tap on the window or anything, and when she looked back a minute later, he was gone.

Sullenly she walked into the entryway. "Thank you, Eliza. I appreciate what you said."

Eliza shook her head. "My son is a good boy, but he still has a thing or two to learn about women!"

That made Lindy laugh in spite of her dark mood. "What would you like me to do now?"

"There are some dishes in the kitchen you can take care of. And if anyone comes into the restaurant, take care of them."

"Sure, Eliza." She walked toward the door of the restaurant and turned around toward Eliza before entering the room. "And thanks again." Nick and Josiah were still sitting at the corner table, and Jenna had joined them. Nick waved her over.

"Sit down for a minute, Lindy, so we can talk to you." Josiah put his coffee down and looked at her. Before she had a chance to sit all the way down, he continued. "Listen, Lindy. I know you're upset about Ray coming to the cave—"

"I'm so sorry, Lindy," said Nick.

Lindy shrugged. "It's not your fault, Nick. I'm just glad you saw him."

"But just because he came to the cave doesn't mean that he can get *here*. I have guards posted there seven twenty-four."

"Twenty-four seven, Josiah," Jenna whispered.

That made Lindy laugh, but she didn't say anything. And the subject was so sobering that the laugh didn't last long. It barely made it to her eyes.

"There is absolutely no way that he can get through, Lindy, without the guard knowing about it. What I'm trying to say is that you're safe here. Brian is safe here."

"Then why did you say it was a good idea that I had a gun? And why do you want Jenna to carry a gun?"

Josiah shook his head, but didn't look at Jenna reproachfully. He didn't look at Jenna at all. If it was Ray, he would have seized the opportunity to make her look stupid—or to hit her.

"All right. There is a slight chance that he could get through the net that we've set up. But the chances are so slim of that happening, and even less that he could get through without anyone knowing."

Jenna spoke up. "Lindy, remember what we talked about? Giving Brian the opportunity to decide the danger for himself? Maybe this is the time to allow that."

Lindy exhaled slowly. "I don't know, Jenna. I just don't know. I'm not comfortable doing that right now. Maybe later, when I get used to the idea of Ray lurking around out there—if I ever do. But definitely not right now."

"Give it some thought, Lindy. Brian loves you very much," said Nick.

Narrowing her eyes, Lindy looked at each of them, and a slight smile touched her lips. "What are all you guys? Brian's cheering section?"

"Add me to that cheering section, Lindy! Whatever a cheering section is. My son is a good man. And if you were planning to marry him before, you shouldn't let that scoundrel ruin your plans. Don't let him win, Lindy!" Eliza stepped into the room, said her piece, and then stepped out again. "That's all I have to say."

Lindy stood up and leaned on the back of the chair where she had sat. She nodded and said, "All I can say is that I'll think about what everyone has said. But right now, I have to get back to work. Thanks for caring about me—and Brian. You're all good friends to both of us." Then she walked into the restaurant kitchen and began doing dishes.

The words that they had said played back in her mind. Was it true—that she and Brian could still be safe here even with Ray running around loose? It scared her. Was it a rational fear or an irrational fear? Lindy knew Ray too well to think that it was an irrational fear. He was capable of anything. He was capable of the worst thing anyone could imagine. No, the fear was realistic.

So the next question, was it an acceptable risk? Maybe she had been too harsh with Brian—calling the whole marriage off. After all, she *had* told him that she would marry him when the issue with Ray was resolved. And the only thing that had changed now was that he had come to the cave. The thought chilled her and brought tears to her eyes. No! She was right with what she had done, and she was going to stick to it!

CHAPTER FORTY-SIX

BRIAN FELT DISTRAUGHT. When he looked in the window hoping that she would see him, she saw him all right. And she immediately looked away. He sighed heavily, climbed into the wagon, and made Dolly trot all the way to his property. Then he felt bad, hugged her, and turned her loose to eat some grass.

Sitting on a tree that he had cut down earlier, he put his head in his hands. He was so close to having happiness again—not that he wasn't happy with his children, he was—but having the love and companionship of a woman was completely different. After Bella died, he had been too busy on the farm and raising the children to even consider falling in love and getting married again. But now, he had fallen in love with Lindy and wanted her to be part of his life.

And what happens? She said that she'd marry him, but now that her ex-husband had turned up—a very violent ex-husband, granted—but he ruined everything! Brian stood up and kicked a small clod of dirt that had been dislodged when the tree fell.

The whole idea of the injustice of it all made him so

angry! He kicked the clod of dirt again, and it went flying. Then he realized what he wanted to do. Since he still had Lindy's gun and the ammunition, he loaded the gun and began shooting. Loading and reloading, he shot until the gun was getting hot, and his finger had a blister. But he was still angry. So he pointed the gun at a squirrel, put his finger on the trigger, but couldn't pull it.

Sinking down into the dirt, he threw the gun, and felt ashamed that he was going to take another creature's life just because he was angry. He thought that killing something would make him feel better, but really, all he wanted to do was kill Ray. After what Ray had done to Lindy, the world would be a better place without him. That made him think about his experiences in the war and how they had changed him. No, he didn't want to kill Ray, regardless of what he had done. Brian didn't want to kill anyone. But he did want to marry Lindy, and she wouldn't marry him because of the scoundrel. There was nothing he could do.

Feeling dejected, Brian picked up the gun and dusted it off. He needed to do something physical to make himself feel better and to get these thoughts out of his head. So he walked back to where the fallen trees were and began sawing off the branches with a smaller saw that he and Nick had bought at the lumber store. As he finished each tree, he dragged the log back to the perimeter of the area where he would build the house. When he had all the logs trimmed and moved, he briefly considered using the chain saw to cut down more trees, but decided that in the mood he was in, it probably wasn't a good idea.

Looking at his work and nodding, he frowned, caught Dolly—who, now that he thought about it, could have run off with all the gunshots, but luckily she didn't—and hooked her up to the wagon. Then he drove slowly into town trying not to think about anything. He left Dolly and the wagon at the livery and walked over to the sheriff's office—the long way, so he wouldn't have to walk in front of the hotel.

As he passed the window, he saw Josiah sitting at his desk. Brian opened the door and stepped inside. "Hey, Josiah," he said without enthusiasm.

"I'm sorry, Brian. I tried talking to her. So did Nick. Even your mother piped up and tried to convince her. But she's not listening to anyone. I'm sorry." Josiah shook his head and looked down.

Brian sank into the chair next to the desk. "Thanks, Josiah."

Nick stepped out of the back room and sat on the edge of the desk. "Hey, Brian. I heard Josiah tell you that we all tried. I'm sorry that she had to hear that. Maybe if —"

"That didn't matter, Nick. She would have heard about it eventually, anyway," said Brian. "You know, I wanted to kill Ray after this morning." He shrugged and shook his head. "But after being in the war, I really don't want to kill anyone. Can't we just catch the scoundrel and turn him in?"

"That would be great, but I don't think it's feasible," said Josiah.

"I feel so helpless," said Brian.

"I know. That jerk has us all running around in circles. He's not that smart, but he's sure besting us." Nick nodded his head.

Brian exhaled quickly. "It's not worth talking about— or thinking about. And I have to stop, or I'll drive myself crazy. Nick, how about if we work on the upstairs?" He motioned up with his head. "That would keep my mind off *Ray* for a while."

"Are you sure you don't want to cut down some more trees at your place? Or trim the branches, or stack them up?"

"The way I feel, I don't think I'd trust myself with a chain saw. But I already trimmed the branches and moved the logs. I'm ready to help you some now. Let's get it done."

"All right then. I had a refreshing morning nap after a long night, and I'm ready to work." Nick stood up.

Josiah stood and walked toward the door. "I don't need to sit here and listen to you boys pounding nails. I'll see you later." And he walked out the door.

"Nick, help me keep my mind off of Ray and *her*. Tell me some jokes or something while we work."

"Will do, mate. Will do," said Nick.

CHAPTER FORTY-SEVEN

LINDY WAS BUSY in the restaurant when Brian came in to pick up his kids. She heard his voice, and he might have stood at the door looking in, but she didn't look over that way, and a few minutes later, his whole family had left. Shortly after that, Eliza came in to relieve her and tell her she could go home. But she stayed a little longer so she could bring supper home to everyone at Nick and Rachel's house. She hoped that Rachel didn't have something else planned, but usually it was a last minute decision, so Lindy thought she was safe.

Walking down the street, carrying her heavy load of meat loaf, mashed potatoes, string beans, and berry pie for six, she felt somehow lighter. Much of the afternoon had been spent—while she was working—thinking about what everyone had said about how safe she was, how much Brian loved her, and especially what Eliza had said about not letting Ray win. That hit her especially hard.

Back when she was married to Ray, he always won. Lindy *hated* that and hated always feeling like a loser when she was around him—a feeling which Ray encouraged with his taunts and insults. No, she wasn't going to let Ray win.

Opening the door of the room with her fragrant packages, she was greeted with, "She did! She brought supper!" Rachel hurried to take the packages from her. "Nick and I were talking about supper and how the last frozen pizza was gone and what were we going to do. Nick thought that you might bring supper when you came from the hotel, and he was right!" Rachel ran up to Nick and kissed him on the cheek. "Good call, big guy!"

"Thanks, wifey," said Nick.

Lindy laughed. "You've been feeding me and Cody all this time, I thought that my turn was seriously overdue. Sorry! But I hope you like this."

"Boys!" Rachel called. "Supper!"

"Mommy!" Cody ran up to her and threw his arms around her.

"Hi, sweetie. Did you have a good day at school?"

Cody nodded. "Yup. I held Amy's hand today!"

"I hope you learned something, too, Cody."

"I did, Mom."

Usually, the boys had eaten first, so the three adults could sit at the table, but this time Nick had to scrounge up a couple more chairs. When they were all seated closely around the table, Nick looked across to Lindy. "Did you have a chance to think about what we all said?"

"Yes, but mostly I thought about what Eliza had said about not letting Ray win." She looked at Rachel and gritted her teeth. "Ray *always* won, and I hated that."

Rachel nodded her head. "And he's winning, now, too."

"I don't want him to. I *really* don't want him to."

"Then don't let him, Lindy. It's up to you," said Nick.

Lindy tightened her lips and nodded to him. And the rest of the conversation at supper was carried by the three boys. When everyone finished eating and telling Lindy how great it was that she brought home supper, Nick retired to the bedroom to get some sleep after his long night at the cave with only a brief nap in the morning, and the boys rushed to the living room to play another board game.

Rachel and Lindy cleaned up the dishes, and as they were finishing, there was a knock at the door. "Who could that be?" asked Rachel as she walked over there.

Lindy hoped that it wasn't Brian. She still had some thinking to do before she saw him again. But when Rachel opened the door, the first words Lindy heard was, "Jenna! Sarah! What a nice surprise! Come on in!" And Lindy felt relieved.

"Lindy! Hi!" said Sarah.

"Hi again, Lindy," said Jenna.

Lindy waved her hand at them. "Hello."

"Come on in. Sit down. Just talk quietly because Nick is trying to get some sleep." Rachel motioned for the women to sit at the table. "To what do we owe this pleasure?"

"Girls' day out!" Sarah leaned across the table and tried to keep her voice down. "We're all going to *town* together!"

"Ryan's going on Saturday instead of Sunday this week, and said he'd cart back our purchases for us. Mary Elizabeth said she doesn't want to go and doesn't mind watching the store because she's in the middle of writing a new novel."

"And we know you don't ride, so Ryan said that you could ride in the wagon with him." Sarah, moving her head up and down excitedly, looked at Lindy.

"Oh, well—" Lindy sat back in the chair and turned her palms face up on the table. "I don't think I can go."

"Why not?" asked Rachel.

"Well, Cody for one."

"Nick will take care of the kids while we're gone. No worries." Rachel patted her hand.

"But Ray—"

"He's already been *here*, Lindy. He won't know you've gone back there," Jenna said.

"And we'll all be with you. He wouldn't dare do anything with all of us there," Sarah said.

"Oh, you don't know Ray like I do."

"Please, Lindy? It will be fun! At least say you'll think about it," pleaded Sarah.

"Come on, we're all going—even Kat. She wants to get some more penicillin," said Jenna.

They all looked at Lindy expectantly. "Okay! I'll think about it!"

CHAPTER FORTY-EIGHT

IT WAS STILL dark when Brian crawled out of bed. He didn't take time to heat the wood stove to make coffee, instead he just pulled his clothes on. Although he hated to wake the children, there was no choice to it. They couldn't stay there alone, that was for sure.

Archie was already awake when he walked into the boy's room, but he had to gently shake Willie. That's all it took, though, and both boys were dressed and ready to go almost immediately. Amy was another story. Brian stood over the sofa where she slept, holding the flickering lantern above her, and watching her sleep. "You boys are going to have to sit in the back and let your sister sleep on your laps, all right?"

"Sure, Pa," both boys agreed.

Brian picked up Amy carefully, trying not to wake her, and they all walked out to the barn. Sitting in the back of the wagon, with Amy on his lap, Willie held the lantern as high as he could, so Brian could hitch up Dolly. Luckily, though, the sky had begun to lighten.

Brian flicked off the lantern and left it in the barn; then they started down the road. By the time they reached the cave, with Amy yawning awake, the sky was ablaze with the color of a beautiful sunrise.

"Hey, there!" called Josiah, when he saw the wagon approaching.

After stopping the wagon, Brian climbed down and approached Josiah. "You sure your horse will be all right following the wagon?"

"Ah, sure! Patches is a good boy who does anything I ask. He'll be fine." Josiah stroked Dolly. "Oh, that reminds me. Ezra asked me to tell you that he got two new horses in, and if you're interested, he'll hold them for you."

Brian thought a minute and then nodded his head vigorously. "Yeah! Tell him to hold both of them for me!"

"Okay, will do." Josiah walked away to retrieve Patches.

As Josiah tied a lead rope from the horse to the back of the wagon, Brian leaned in and said, "You children going to be all right back here?"

"Yes, Papa," said Willie.

"Amy, do you want to ride up front with Sheriff Josiah?"

Amy, still half asleep and with her thumb uncharacteristically in her mouth, nodded. "Yes, Papa."

Brian lifted her out, waited for Josiah to climb aboard, and then lifted Amy up to him. When he stepped back and smiled, Amy said, "Thanks, Papa," and then snuggled into Josiah, who put his arm around her.

"Don't worry, Papa, I'll take good care of your children," said Josiah, smiling.

"Bye, boys, bye, Amy. See ya, Josiah, and don't forget to tell Ezra that I'm interested!"

Josiah shook the reins, and the wagon took off with Patches trailing willingly behind. Brian watched them go and smiled. It was a good place to live, and he and Lindy and the children would have a good life here. His smile faded. As soon as Ray was dealt with.

Then he thought of the horses again and perked right up. His own horse, maybe two! He liked the idea of that. The more he thought about it, the more he liked it. Then he thought about something else—something that went along with getting a horse. And he liked that idea, too. All the ideas ran around in his head and kept him busy for hours.

He had been sitting on a rock, but when he heard hoofbeats approaching, he quickly stood up and held the rifle at the ready, with his finger on the trigger. When he realized that the hoofbeats were from this side of the cave, he put the rifle down. When he saw the rider, a big grin spread across his face. "Nick! I *wanted* to talk to you!"

"Thought you might need some of this." Nick slid off his horse and handed Brian a container of some sort that felt warm to the touch.

"What is it?" He held it up to his ear and shook it.

"Stop shaking it! Open the lid by twisting. And don't let Josiah see it! He'd never approve of a to-go cup."

Brian twisted the top off and smelled the dark liquid inside. "Coffee! Thank you!" He took a big swallow and cried out, "Ow! It's hot!"

"That's what a to-go cup does—it keeps liquids hot for you. Are you okay?"

"Ah, yeah, but I think I'll wait until it cools off to try that again. I burned my tongue." Brian twisted the cap back on.

"It won't cool for a long time if you leave the cap on, Brian. Take it off."

After Brian untwisted the cap again, he held up the container. "You know, I want one of these. Several. I'll keep them away from Josiah. That's what I want to talk to you about, Nick. Can we go back *there*? I have some things that I want to buy."

"Yeah, that's a great idea, Brian. After we worked on the upstairs yesterday, I realized there were many things that I still need—like doors. I need to buy some and bring them back. Do you want doors for your place?"

"No, I think I'd rather make them myself. Can we go tomorrow?"

"I'm on watch tonight, but if I can fall asleep by seven and you wake me by ten, we should have plenty of time." Nick hopped back on his horse. "What do you want to get there, anyway?"

"More building supplies. I know we can go back there anytime, but I'd feel better if it was all here when I was ready for it. And didn't you tell me that Ryan has some interesting"—he whispered—"twenty-first-century"—he went back to his normal tone of voice—"items? I want to get some so Lindy will feel more at home."

"You'll have to be vigilant about keeping them away from Josiah. Although Jenna has a cell phone and some other electronics, and they have some solar electric devices in their house. Didn't they leave any of them at the house?"

"No, just the flickering lanterns. I want some of those, too. Oh! And a flashing light."

"Flashlight." Nick corrected.

"All right. Flashlight. I'd like one of those. And some games for the children. Willie and Archie couldn't stop

204

talking about the games they played at your house."

Nick laughed. "Anything else you want over there?"

"Yeah," Brian said. "A puppy."

CHAPTER FORTY-NINE

WHEN LINDY ARRIVED at the hotel in the morning for work, Brian's children were in the restaurant eating breakfast. He was nowhere to be seen, and she didn't ask where he was. But she heard the children talking about the big rifle that he carried, so she figured he was on guard duty at the cave.

She tried not to think that he was there for her, that all of them were on guard duty *for her*. If she kept thinking about that she would feel so guilty that she couldn't go on. So she chose to keep it out of her thoughts. If she didn't, it would drive her crazy, so she focused on her work. Instead she thought about going to *town* with the girls. Girls' day out, Sarah had called it. The thought of it made her smile.

But she still wasn't sure if it was a good idea for her to go where Ray could easily find her. Although he had already found her here, so she wasn't sure that it mattered. Still, the thought of going out *there* made her feel even more vulnerable than she already felt. Ray may have already been here, but still, she felt a certain amount of safety—the small town feel of the place, the sheriff wearing a gun on his hip, everyone looking out for her. They all cared about her. What a great feeling that was!

So why should she even go there when she felt so great here? Because they wanted her to go. Sarah had said that it would be fun. Lindy knew that she could definitely use a little fun in her life. The last few days had been intense. Was she actually thinking of going? Her eyes opened a little wider at the thought of it while she did the morning dishes. No, she was still undecided. Yes, definitely undecided. That made her smile.

When she finished with the dishes, the children had gone off to school, and everyone in the restaurant had left, she wandered out to the front desk to catch up with Eliza. Jenna was there with Milo talking to her.

"I can't, Jenna, really." Eliza shook her head and didn't look up.

"Come on, Eliza. You've only been there once. Come and see more! You'll like it!"

"No, Jenna, I don't think so," said Eliza.

Lindy just stood back and didn't want to interrupt the discussion. But she didn't say anything, either.

"Eliza, you'll have such a great time!"

Eliza shrugged, shook her head, and said, "Mmm-mmm."

Then Jenna noticed that Lindy was standing there. "Even Lindy is going! Aren't you, Lindy?" asked Jenna while looking Lindy straight in the eye and nodding her head up and down.

"Um, yes. I guess I am going. Yes," said Lindy, surprising herself by agreeing.

Eliza looked up, surprised. "You *are*?" Lindy nodded. "I thought you'd be afraid—"

207

Jenna interrupted. "We'll be with her. She doesn't have to be afraid of anything there. We're going to go and have a fun time. And you're coming with us, Eliza!"

Eliza tilted her head and looked at Jenna with half a grimace, half a smile on her face. "Well, all right. If you insist—as long as we're not gone too long."

Jenna smiled broadly. "Only as long it takes! I'm go tell Sarah that you and Lindy are going! She'll be surprised!" And she waltzed out of the hotel while Lindy and Eliza looked on.

"I do believe that we've been rooked! Can you finish back here, Lindy? I need to talk to Samuel about this. He will be none too happy, I'm afraid." She shook her head. "And neither am I." Eliza walked out from behind the front desk and into her sitting room.

As Lindy did the work behind the front desk, Granny and Edward came down the stairs, holding hands as usual. "Hi, Granny, Edward!"

"Hallo, dear. How are you on this fine day?"

"Fine. How are you doing?"

"I'm holding hands with my bride, aren't I? How could I be anything but fine?" He smiled.

Granny pulled her hand away from his and pushed him away. "You old fart! You're just saying that to get into my good graces!"

"I thought I already got into your good graces, dear." Edward smiled and raised his eyebrows at her.

"Oh, tarnation!" Granny said and put her arm around him.

"Are you going to *town* with us, Granny?" asked Lindy.

Granny leaned against the front desk. "I'll tell you what, Lindy. Since I moved here more than a year ago, I've been back once. For this." She pointed to her heart.

208

"And I ain't going back. Ever. This is where my life is"— she looked at Edward with love in her eyes—"and my love, and I have no need to go back ever. Not interested. There's nothing for me there. I have one great-grand-daughter there, but she comes here often enough to suit me." Before Lindy could respond, Granny looked at Edward. "You ready to go to the saloon for drink, big boy?"

"A sarsaparilla would suit me fine," said Edward.

"That's exactly what I was thinking!" Granny cackled with laughter, and the two of them walked out, arm in arm.

Lindy had a break right before lunch time, and she ate a quick meal in the restaurant before a few people wandered in. Since the decision to go to the girls' day out had already been made, her thoughts turned to Brian, and if she should tell him that he knew the risks and that she would go along with whatever he decided. Of course, she knew what he would decide. Still, should she tell him that?

Maybe she should just leave it alone, and maybe he would find someone else, and she wouldn't have to worry about it anymore. That thought unexpectedly shot a pain like an arrow through her heart. No, she definitely didn't want him to find someone else. Okay, that much was decided. But whether she should leave the decision up to him or not still confused her. For now, her focus would be on getting up the courage to go on the girls' day out, since she had already committed herself to going. Maybe she and Eliza could huddle in a corner somewhere while the other women did their thing.

The children came in from school, running around and laughing, and it made her smile. Lindy loved children, and Brian's children were wonderful kids. She wouldn't mind at all being their stepmother. She watched as the children ran around and settled down when Eliza asked them to. Still no sign of Brian, so her assessment that he was on guard duty was probably correct. When it was time to leave, she decided to bring supper home again for everyone. They would love tonight's meal of lamb chops, beets, and peach pie.

CHAPTER FIFTY

BRIAN WAS SO excited about the upcoming trip to *town* that he woke up before sunrise. His mind drifted back to how the previous day had ended. It had been a long, boring day—except for his conversation with Nick—and Brian had to walk around to keep from dozing off. Then Nick arrived back at the cave, with the children in the wagon, and Nick's horse following placidly behind. Although Brian was glad to see the kids and hug them and kiss them after the long absence, he would have preferred if Nick had left them at the hotel. Because Brian really wanted to go see Ezra about the horses. But instead, Brian drove Dolly home with his children already fed, and his mother having sent along a packet of food for him. She was so thoughtful. And it was so good to be home.

After those thoughts drifted from his mind, he tried falling asleep again, but to no avail. So he decided to go over what he expected the day would bring. After dropping off the children at the hotel, he would walk over—rush over was more like it—to the livery to talk to Ezra. He could hardly wait to try out the two horses! His own land, his own horses, and with any luck after Ray was taken care of, his own wife. He already had a family, but it didn't seem complete without a wife to go with it. And he had completely forgotten! He already had those little horses for the children! They will love those.

Before he could go over the rest of the day in his head, Archie had come into the room and snuggled in beside him. Brian wrapped his arms around him and kissed him on the top of his head. Sometimes he forgot what a little boy his middle child still was. After their mother died, the two older children had to take on more responsibility at the cost of their childhood. Only Amy—who was too young for any responsibility anyway—was spared the loss of her young childhood. He was glad they still had time left to just be children. And he could hardly wait to see their faces when he brought home games from *there*. They'll love them!

It wasn't long before Willie and then Amy came in to his bedroom. With all three children there, he wasn't going to get any more sleep, so he encouraged them to get off the bed, and then he got up. Brian often made breakfast, but today he decided they could eat at the hotel again. His mother didn't mind—he thought she enjoyed doting on them. It was so sad that she wasn't able to be around for their first years, but he was grateful that he was here now, and she could enjoy them every day.

After driving to town and accompanying the children inside to his mother's loving care, he rushed out the door, and was so excited about the prospect of looking at the horses, that he ran all the way to the livery. He forced himself not to look in the direction of the house Lindy was staying in. She would reconsider when she was ready to, and until then, he would wait for her. Not exactly patiently, but he *would* wait. Brian ran into the livery, calling out "Ezra! Ezra!" and all the while looking into each stall to see where the new horses were.

"Right here, Brian. Guess you want to see the new horses, huh?" Ezra strolled out from the back with his fingers stuck in the pockets of his jeans and a smile on his face.

"Yes, I do! You didn't sell them, did you?" asked Brian, fearful that he was too late.

Ezra shook his head. "Told Josiah I'd keep 'em for you, and I did. I'll get them now."

As Brian waited, he turned around and discovered that he was in front of the stalls with his little horses in them. He patted them all, and they were all very sweet. When everything in his life quieted down a little, he'd show them to the children and start teaching them to ride.

Ezra still hadn't come out with the horses, so Brian thought about what he'd want the horses to look like. Well, his horse. He would be tall and white, because he wanted Lindy to see him riding tall and proud on a big, white horse. With that thought, he heard Ezra coming, and he turned around.

Ezra led two horses, one tall, white one, and one shorter bay, with a long, black forelock and a beautiful face. "I wasn't sure how well you rode, Brian, since you always take the wagon, so I didn't know which one you might want. The white one is a little more spirited, though responsive if you want him to slow down. And he's a gelding. The bay mare was apparently an older child's horse, so very gentle. Which one are you interested in?"

213

"Possibly both, but I'll try this one first." Brian petted the head of the white horse and opened his mouth to look at his teeth.

"He's still a young horse, plenty of years to go. This one's young also. I think they might be related. Oh! Which reminds me. These two are a different kind of horse than you might be used to. They come from Missouri. You know where that is?"

"We traveled through there on our way home. Why are they different just because they come from Missouri?"

"They call them fox trotters, and they have a really smooth gait. Wait till you get on him. I'll saddle him up for you."

While Ezra went to get the saddle, Brian stroked both horses and checked the bay's mouth. He loved them both already! And he hoped that riding the big, white one was all he wanted it to be. After helping Ezra brush both horses, he held the big, white one while Ezra saddled him.

Then Brian climbed on and asked the horse out to the dirt street. At first they walked down the street, but when Brian made an encouraging sound with his mouth, the horse sped up. He could tell that the horse was rarin' to go. The gait that the horse broke into wasn't a trot, but it was faster than a walk. And it was the smoothest horse that Brian had ever ridden. If the mare was this smooth, she would be perfect for Lindy! As he rode back to the livery, he couldn't believe how smooth the horse was. Then he got off and climbed on the other horse, which Ezra had already saddled.

Ezra shook his head. "You know, Brian, that horse is too small for you. I didn't realize how tall you are."

214

"I'm not buying her for myself. I'm buying her for Lindy, and she's short!" Brian asked the horse to walk outside, and when they got to the dirt street, he asked her to go faster. She was calmer than the other horse, but she still did everything that Brian asked. When he returned to the livery, he swung out of the saddle. "I'll take them both! This one *is* perfect for Lindy!"

"All right, but I should have warned you before-hand. These two are expensive. Missouri Fox Trotters are hard to come by."

"How much?" asked Brian.

"I'd need twenty-five for each of them. If you don't have that much all at once, we can work out a payment plan."

Brian reached into his pockets which were bulging with coins that he expected to use today—forgetting about the differences of twenty-first-century money. He counted out fifty dollars and paid Ezra. Then he gave him fifty more to pay for board for the little horses and for these two.

"All right, Brian. That will last a while."

"I hope to have them out at my own place before long. I still have to build it, though!" Brian swung back up on the tall, white horse and started riding him out the door.

"Hey, Brian?"

Brian turned around. "Yeah, Ezra. Did I forget something?"

"Were you going to bring Dolly and the wagon over this morning?"

"Oh! I completely forgot. We're going somewhere later, but she would be none too happy with me if I didn't get her fed before we left." He started to swing off the white horse.

"Wait! Before you get off. I wouldn't say this about many horses, but Dolly is the sweetest horse I've met. I'll get you a lead. You can lead her—wagon and all—and then ride your new horse some more."

"Great! Thanks, Ezra!" While he waited for Ezra to bring him the lead, he thought about what to name the big horse. Then he remembered what Ezra had said about the horse being spirited. "Spirit!" he said, stroking the horse on the broad neck. "Your name's Spirit!"

Ezra handed him the lead rope, and horse and rider walked out the entrance to the livery and straight up the street.

CHAPTER FIFTY-ONE

LINDY STEPPED OUT the door to walk to the hotel and immediately heard hoof beats. It was an odd, rhythmical sound, though. When she got past the house, she turned her head to look, and it was a man on a tall, white horse approaching. Then she realized it was Brian! Her heart gave a lurch, and she stumbled into the street. He stopped the horse right in front of her, but it danced around in the street before he got it to stand still.

"How do you like my new horse?"

"He's beautiful," said Lindy. What she didn't say was "and you are, too." She couldn't get over how wonderful he looked sitting atop that horse.

"Lindy," he said, looking serious, "I bought one for you, too—for after we're married."

"I don't know how to ride."

"I'll teach you, just like I taught you to shoot." She nodded, and he continued. "I bought horses—small ones —for the children, too, including Cody. I'll teach you all to ride together. All right?"

All she could do was nod and murmur "Okay."

"Lindy, I love you, and I'll wait for you for as long as it

takes. Do you understand that? I'm waiting for you—no matter what you say. I'm waiting for *you*."

"You know it can't be—"

"Yes, I know. Let's not talk about that. It will happen when it happens. So, will you still marry me?"

Lindy exhaled slowly and nodded. "Yes, Brian, I will. But I still won't associate with you until *then*." If he didn't want her to mention Ray, she wouldn't, but she wanted him to know her terms.

"Fair enough!"

Then he nodded to her, and the horse walked down the street in a weird manner. Lindy didn't know much about horses, but she knew that horse walked in a weird way! It was fast, but strange. Then she wondered if *her* horse walked funny like that. Her horse. Those were words that she never thought she'd be saying. *Her* horse. *Her* husband. But it all depended on Ray being out of their lives, and there was no telling how long that would take.

As she walked up the street, she watched as Brian attached a rope to Dolly, the horse that was in front of the wagon. Before she reached the hotel, they had all walked away, wagon and all. When she opened the door of the hotel and looked back, they had turned the corner and were gone.

"Did Brian just drive the wagon away?" Eliza stood behind the front desk and looked up when Lindy opened the door.

"Well, he didn't exactly drive it away as ride it away," said Lindy.

"Ride it away? Whatever do you mean by that?"

"He bought a new horse. He attached a rope to the horse in front of the wagon and led her off!"

"Brian bought himself a horse? Well, that's good. He's got the money, it's time he buys himself some of his own things." Eliza moved some papers around and then looked up again. "What color is the horse?"

"White."

Jenna stepped out from her room. "So your white knight came riding up on a white horse to save you, huh, Lindy?"

Lindy nodded. "Yeah, I guess he did."

"White knight on a white horse? What are you two going on about?" asked Eliza.

"I'll explain it later, Eliza. Right now, Sarah and I are going to start making plans for our big outing tomorrow. Is there anywhere special either of you two ladies would like to go?" When they both shook their heads "no" Jenna, carrying Milo, walked out the door.

"I don't even want to go," said Eliza.

"I don't either," said Lindy.

"Will you still go, then?" Eliza looked at her with raised eyebrows.

"Yeah, I said I would. You?"

Eliza nodded. "I suppose I will." After a minute of silence, Eliza said, "Lindy, you want to finish up back here, then take care of the restaurant? Can you cook breakfast for anyone who comes in and do the dishes as well? I need to get some work done in the house."

"Sure, Eliza. I can handle it."

When Eliza turned to walk into her sitting room, Lindy stepped into the restaurant and wondered what Eliza had to do in there that was so important. Lindy didn't mind handling the restaurant all by herself, but Eliza had never asked that before, so she thought it was a little strange.

Lindy filled up the coffee for the two patrons who were in the restaurant, and then cleaned up the table where Brian's children had eaten breakfast. They were now at a corner table playing cards. They waved to her when they saw her, and she smiled and waved back. She wondered what it would be like to be a mother of four children instead of one. They were good, well-mannered kids, she'd have to give them that. Brian did a good job of raising them mostly by himself. If—no, when—she was their mother, she would love them, every one.

Now, she wanted to keep her distance from them—the same distance that she wanted to keep with Brian. Until Ray was caught—if he ever was—she wasn't going to associate with Brian at all. Accidentally meeting him on the street, like she did this morning, was as close as she wanted to get. Well, she wanted to get closer, but she wouldn't allow it. It was better for everyone if she stayed away.

Then she thought about what Jenna had said about Brian being a white knight riding a white horse. She loved the image, and it wasn't one that she would soon forget. He looked so handsome up there! Although she'd stay away from him, she felt like she was falling deeper and deeper in love with him every day.

CHAPTER FIFTY-TWO

AFTER BRIAN DELIVERED Dolly and the wagon to the livery, he rode Spirit all around town several times. Then, since he still had plenty of time, he gaited him all the way out to his new land. If he had more time, he thought, he'd ride the perimeter of the property. He could do that tomorrow. On the way back, he wanted to see how well the horse could gallop, and the answer was, that he had a fast, smooth gallop that anyone would be happy about. Brian *loved* his new horse! He couldn't be happier about buying him. When he arrived back at the livery, as soon as he saw Ezra, he said, "Ezra! He's great! I love him! Thanks so much! Would you put him up for me?"

Ezra nodded, laughed, and took the reins as Brian dismounted. "Glad you like him, Brian. I had a feeling that horse had your name on it!"

Brian shook Ezra's hand and stroked the big horse's neck several times before he walked outside, up the street, and around the corner to the general store. He had tried to time it just right to spend some time in the store before walking next door and waking Nick. When

221

he walked in and saw Ryan, he was about to say hello when Ryan spoke first.

"Brian! Glad you stopped by! I wanted to ask you a favor. The girls wanted me to take them to town tomorrow, but it's my day to stand guard. I usually go to town on Sunday—that's why the days are messed up. But anyway, any chance that you'll switch with me? You do tomorrow and I'll do Sunday?"

"Uh, girls?"

"Oh, you know. Jenna, Sarah, Eliza, and my sister Kat is going, too. Mary Elizabeth doesn't want to go because she's in the middle of writing her new novel. And oh, yeah, Lindy is going, too."

"Lindy is going?" That surprised Brian.

"Well, Jenna said that she had to do some fast talking to get Eliza and Lindy to go, but she managed to convince them, somehow." Ryan shrugged. "You know how persuasive my sister can be."

"Sure, I can do that for you. And it works out perfectly, because I came over here to ask you a favor." Brian looked around the store to make sure no one else was there. "No one in the back?"

"Mary Elizabeth's upstairs working, but nobody else. What's up?"

"I want you to show me the twenty-first-century things that you have. I'm planning for my new house—and I want Lindy to feel more at home there—you know."

"Well, sure, what do you want to see?"

"Everything!" said Brian enthusiastically.

"Let's go upstairs." Ryan came out from behind the counter and waved his arm at Brian. "Follow me."

"Where's your dog today?"

"Bear likes to sleep at Mary Elizabeth's feet when she

works. Come on up."

Brian didn't know what to expect, but he felt excited to see anything that Ryan had to show him. As he was stepping up the final few steps before entering the upstairs, he heard a funny tapping noise.

"Mary Elizabeth, sorry to disturb you. Have you met Brian yet?" Ryan put his hand on her shoulder.

"Oh, hmmm, hi, Brian," she said without looking up.

The tapping sound was coming from a strange instrument. As her fingers hit the little buttons, something would strike the paper and make a mark on it. When he looked again, he found that he could read it. "Hi, Mary Elizabeth."

"She's typing," said Ryan.

"Is that—?"

Ryan laughed. "No, that has already been invented here, but not in general supply yet. I wanted her to use this"—he walked over to something on the kitchen table —"but she insisted on using something more period appropriate."

"What's this?" Brian looked at a rectangular object on the kitchen table that didn't look like it did much. Then Ryan opened it up, and the whole front of it lit up.

"This is a computer. Almost everyone in the twenty-first century has one. You can type on here just like Mary Elizabeth does there"—he pointed to her—"but with this you'd have to print it out on that." Ryan walked over to a counter and placed his hand on a bigger rectangle that looked completely different from the "computer" on the table. "The way that it works is that you type something out on there and then plug this in—in the twenty-first century you don't have to plug it in, but that's too complicated to explain—and then this prints it out for you. What Mary Elizabeth is doing is printing it out as she goes."

"Do you think Lindy would need a computer?"

"Do you know if she had one over *there*?" asked Ryan.

"I don't know," admitted Brian.

"Tell you what. You and Nick are going today right?" Brian nodded. "Don't get one. Then I'll ask her tomorrow, and I'll pick one up for you—for her. Or, you can get it another time."

Brian shook his head. "You can pick it up tomorrow, if you don't mind. I just feel like I want it to be mine—I don't know—maybe the money will run out or something. I want it all now."

"From what I heard, your money isn't going to run out for a good long time!"

"So what else can you show me? Do you have a flashing light?"

Ryan smiled. "A flashlight. Yeah, over here." He opened a drawer, took out a long cylindrical object, and then pushed a button on the side. It lit up! "Here. Take a look."

Brian turned it off and on, then pointed it to his face, turned it on, and quickly closed his eyes and then blinked repeatedly. "That's bright!"

"Not all of them are this bright. Take a look and get one just like it if you like the brightness. And be sure to get rechargeable batteries. Oh! And take a look at this." He held up another object with removable pieces in it. "This is a solar battery charger. See? You put the batteries in here, and the sun charges them up. You can use them over and over. It's cool!"

"What are batteries?"

"They make it work. You'll need batteries."

"Yeah, then I need one of those for sure. What else?"

"You are eager for the twenty-first century, aren't you? You don't want to move there, do you?"

"No! I love it right here. When I visited there, it was all right, but I prefer it here. Quieter. Slower. More peaceful. I hope Lindy does, too. What else?"

"Come over here. I have several of these. They are miniature solar collectors. You can plug stuff into them. See here? I have the refrigerator plugged in."

"What's a refrigerator?"

"You know what an ice box is? Have you seen one?"

"Yeah. Back in the East, some people had them."

Ryan opened the door of the refrigerator. "Stick your hand in there."

"It's cold!"

"Yes, it keeps food cold for you. It's very handy. You'd have to hide it, though. The only reason that Josiah doesn't go ballistic about this is because we don't allow anyone to go upstairs. So it's safe."

"I could build a secret room onto the house!"

Ryan laughed. "I think that would be perfect, Brian. Josiah would probably agree to that—though he'd probably want you to keep a lock on it!"

"I definitely want one of these. It would come in really handy, I think."

"And there's one last thing that I'm sure you'll want—maybe even several of them." Ryan walked into the bedroom and returned with a small device that he handed to Brian. "Put your finger there and touch that little symbol on the screen. Now push the little arrow."

Brian watched and the picture on the screen started moving. "It's Mary Elizabeth riding a horse!"

"It's a video. There are all kinds of them. Now push

225

that. Then put your finger there. This is a PacMan game —it's old, but people still enjoy it. I do. Don't let that guy eat you! Oh, too late. Anyway, that's just one game on there, and there are several. This device can do all kinds of things. Several of us have them. If Lindy didn't have one over *there*, she wanted one. So I'd definitely get at least one of them."

"What's it called?"

"This is an iPad, I think they're the best, but you can get any tablet out there and it will do similar things."

"I'll get an iPad. I'll get several!"

"Hey! Anybody home?" called a voice from downstairs, that Brian recognized as Nick.

"We'll be right down, Nick. That's about it, Brian. And as you're buying this stuff, you might see more that interests you." He leaned down and kissed Mary Elizabeth as he walked by. "Bye, sweetie. Sorry we disturbed you." She nodded without looking up, and Brian followed Ryan back downstairs.

CHAPTER FIFTY-THREE

THE MORNING FLEW by, and Lindy couldn't even say what she had done. The only thoughts in her head were of a white knight riding a white horse, and the knight's face looked like Brian's. Although the thought had been circulating in her head all morning, it still made her smile every time the vision appeared in her mind's eye. With Eliza in her own quarters all morning, Lindy took care of everything. When she got busy, she didn't call out for Eliza, she just dealt with it on her own. And now the rush was over, and she sat at the far end of the restaurant close to the front door of the hotel, in case someone came in, and enjoyed a cup of coffee.

She turned when she heard footsteps coming. It was Eliza, with a funny look on her face.

"Hi, Eliza. You okay?"

"Yes, I'm fine, dear. You've done a great job today. You didn't even ask for my help once. Thank you for that. I needed to get the house cleaned up for tomorrow."

"Are you having company?"

"No. You know. Because we're going *there*."

"Oh, the girls' day out, you mean. But why do you have to clean the house for *that*?"

Eliza looked down at her hands in her lap. "So it's clean for Samuel when I'm gone."

Lindy laughed. "Eliza, we're only going to be gone for the day! You make it sound like we're not coming back!"

When Eliza looked up at Lindy, she had tears sliding down her face. "I've had a feeling all along that once there, I won't be able to get back." She looked around, her eyes sweeping the restaurant and as much of the hotel as she could see from her chair. "Samuel's had the same feeling. He's begged me not to go."

"Then don't go, Eliza. And I won't go, either!" Lindy softly put her fist on the table.

Just then, Jenna walked in. "Hello, ladies! Are you both ready for a fun day tomorrow? We're going to have a blast! See ya later, then!" And she strolled out just as she had strolled in.

Eliza shook her head and said quietly, "We have to go, Lindy. We have to go." They both sat there in stunned silence for a few minutes, and then Eliza stood up. You can have a break now, Lindy. You've worked really hard today, handling everything by yourself. Thank you for that. Take a couple of hours off. More if you'd like. And eat something before you go. I'll be in there if you need me. But you need a break. Take a good chunk of time off. I don't want to see you back here anytime soon!" Her lips formed a smile that Lindy could tell was forced, and then Eliza walked out of the room.

Lindy sat there a minute thinking about what Eliza had said. Was the cave unstable or something? She didn't remember ever hearing anything like that. Jenna, Ryan, and Rachel had all been coming and going in and out of the cave for more than a year. A hunger pang disturbed her thoughts, so she shrugged, walked into the kitchen to make herself a quick sandwich, and walked out of the hotel.

Although she didn't know where she was going, she turned left as she stepped out the door. The house and the school were that way, but she wasn't going to either of those places. It was like her feet had a mind of their own. A few minutes later, she smiled when she realized where she was: in front of the livery.

"Hallo, young lady! What can I help you with today?" asked a lanky man with a smile.

"I, um, my fi—um, my friend, Brian, said he bought me a horse." Lindy didn't know anything about horses or horse people, and she felt uncomfortable there. Although all her friends were horse people, so she chided herself that she should just relax. They're like everybody else.

"Oh! I know just the one. The cute little Fox Trotter mare." He turned around quickly and said, "I'm Ezra! C'mon back, I'll show you."

"Hi, Ezra, I'm Lindy."

"Hallo, Lindy! C'mon!" Ezra walked fast, and she had to push herself to keep up with him.

Lindy followed him back and passed several ponies on the way. She cleared her throat. "Um, Ezra? Are these the ponies that Brian bought, too?"

Ezra stopped and turned around. "Those two there are Nick's boys' horses. These four here are for Brian's children. He hasn't brought them in to see them yet, though. Not sure what he's waiting for." He walked to the next stall. "Anyway, here's the pretty little mare that's for you. If you need anything else, lemme know," he said and turned and walked through a door in the back.

The horse put its head over the gate, and Rachel petted its pretty face. Although she didn't understand it, she felt something in her heart give way. The horse was brown with a black mane and tail. The mane hung down between the ears, over the top of her head, and covered her eyes. Lindy pushed the mane away and looked into the soft brown eyes. "Could you love me, too? I hope so, because I love you already." She stood there for a few minutes feeling a peace wash over her entire body. My horse, she thought. Glancing over at the stall next to the mare's, she saw the big, white horse that Brian had been riding earlier. And my white knight riding his white horse. A smile spread across her face, and she took a deep breath relishing the horsey air.

CHAPTER FIFTY-FOUR

"THIS CAVE GIVES me the woolies!" said Brian, wrapping his arms around himself and moving uncomfortably from side to side. "I don't care if I *ever* go through it again!"

Nick looked at him, dumbfounded. "You don't want to go *home*?"

Brian slapped him on the arm. "Oh, Nick! Of course! I meant *after* we go back!"

"Dude! I thought maybe you'd lost your mind or something!" After a few minutes of silence, Nick said, "So you know what you want to get here? Where you want to go?"

"I've got a lot on my list." Brian started silently counting the places out on his fingers.

"We don't have to do them all today, right?"

"I was serious, Nick. I never want to come back here—never want to have to go through that cave again."

"Okay. We'll get as much done as we can then, and if Zack is home and he finished, we'll collect the rest of your money."

"I still need to pay you."

"Let's wait and see how much twenty-first-century money you spend today, and then we'll figure it all out after that."

Zack wasn't at the ranch house when they got there, so they put the cooler in the back seat of Nick's truck, and headed out. "Where first?" asked Nick.

"I'd like to get some games for the kids—they really enjoy the ones at your house."

"First stop, Toys'R'Us!"

After Nick parked the truck, they walked into a huge store stuffed full with toys. They walked past row after row of toys, with the shelves head-high filled with more toys. Thirty minutes later, they walked out with an over-flowing basketful of games, some stuffed animals, including two for Cody, and some balls and baseball equipment. Nick told Brian that it would be popular in a few years, and Brian wanted to be prepared. He bought a football and a basketball, too, for good measure.

"We made good time with that, considering that you practically bought out the whole store!"

"Given more time, I think I probably could have done a better job." Both men laughed.

"Where next?" asked Nick.

"I'd like to get all the solar objects that Ryan had."

"Okay, that place is at the edge of town. You'll see some of the new Red Bluff that you haven't seen before."

The rest of the morning and the beginning of the afternoon flew by with Nick's truck getting fuller with every stop. Brian winced after they left the lumber store and stashed a huge load of tools in the back seat. Several of Nick's doors stuck out the back of the truck.

"I don't know about you, Brian, but I'm starved. But

if you want to try to find puppies, we need to hurry. So I'm making a management decision and"—Nick put on his blinker—"and we're going to eat here. But *please*, don't tell Rachel or Lindy that I took you here!"

Fifteen minutes later, their bellies full of what Nick called hamburger, fries, and a chocolate shake, they returned to the ranch house. Zack was home. Before they went in, they loaded the wagon with everything from the truck, and when it didn't look like it would hold anymore, they added the last two chair-desks to the top. Then they knocked on the door and entered the house.

"Hey, guys. I saw you loading the wagon. You sure got quite a haul!" Zack invited them into the living room.

"Brian, here, never wants to come back here. So he bought everything he might ever want! That's including electronics, solar, and lumber, and don't forget—puppies." Nick sat down on the couch.

"Puppies? What kind of puppies?" asked Zack.

Madison walked out from the back. "Did I hear some-one say puppies? I have a friend who's dog had a litter a few weeks ago." She looked up at the ceiling and put her hand to her mouth. "If I could only remember who it was."

"What kind do you want?" asked Zack.

"I'm not particular. All puppies are cute, and they all grow up to be dogs. I'm sure whatever your friend has will be fine—if you can remember which friend!" Brian laughed.

"I'll go make some calls!" Madison disappeared out of the room.

"Hey, Zack. I hate to ask this. But would it be too much to ask to do a shower?"

"Do a shower?" asked Zack.

"He means take a shower! Brian bought a solar shower—just in case—but now he wants to know if he shouldn't have," said Nick.

"Sure, sure. Come in here." Zack walked from the room motioning Brian to follow. When they were in the bathroom, Zack pointed to the toilet. "You know how that works, right? Put the seat up, flush when you're finished, and put the seat back down—otherwise Madison will have a cow."

"A cow?"

"Ah, forget it, Brian, just be sure to put the seat down. Anyway, here is where you turn on the shower and where you adjust the hot and cold settings. If you're not sure, don't step in until it's adjusted, and step out before you turn it off. There's soap and shampoo there. And here's a towel. Enjoy!"

"Thanks, Zack!" Fifteen minutes later, Brian walked out rubbing his hair with the towel. "That was refreshing!"

"Brian, let's get all the money straight before you leave, okay?" Zack, with paper and pencil in front of him, looked at Brian.

"Sure. The only twenty-first-century money I need is what I currently owe Nick."

"Nick, can you give me a figure?" asked Zack.

"Can I borrow that?" Nick pointed to the pencil and paper. When Zack handed him a fresh sheet of paper, he wrote some figures down. Then he added them up and handed the paper to Zack. "Here. If you have old west money, I'll take it in that. I won't be back here for a while, either. Brian and I are adding an upstairs to the sheriff's office."

"All right. Give me a minute." Zack referred to Nick's

paper, wrote down some numbers, and then walked out of the room. When he returned, he carried bags of coins. "Madison and I took another trip to the city to get all this. We've got finals, and I don't want to deal with it for a while." He made several more trips until there were stacks of bags in front of Nick, and three times as many in front of Brian. "All right. That makes us even. Now, would you mind if I gave you more bags to take back and divvy up for me? I made this ledger"—he handed them a red ledger—"so you can keep track, and I'll give you this book"—he held up a red coin book—"and someone else can deal with it for now."

"Sure, we can do that," said Nick. "I don't know if we can cart all that cash back with us right now, though. How about if you give the other bags to Ryan and the girls tomorrow?"

"They're coming tomorrow and not Sunday? Yeah, sure, I can do that."

"I don't know how we're going to get all this in the wagon as it is. It's loaded pretty tight right now."

"How about if Madison and I load it all up while you guys go look at puppies?"

"Yeah, I found some puppies for you, Brian. They're half collie, half shepherd. Is that okay with you?"

Brian shrugged. "Perfect, I guess."

"Here's the address, Nick." Madison handed Nick a sheet of paper. "You know how to get there?"

"Yeah, no problem. Let's go, Brian. I'm eager to get this done and get back home. We've been gone a long time."

The puppies were at a small house, next to a lot of other small houses. Nick called it a housing development and said he didn't like that. Brian didn't either. It made him appreciate the hundred sixty acres that he just bought.

After ringing the doorbell, they walked into a back room with a big fluffy dog. "That's a collie," said Nick, "in case you've never seen one." The dog came up to Brian and licked his hand, making him smile.

"Here are the puppies over here," said the woman who led the way to a box in the corner. "They were sleeping, but it's okay to wake them."

Brian knelt down, looked at the six puppies, and picked up one black puppy and held it to his face. The puppy licked him. "He is wonderful!"

"The puppies are only six weeks old and not ready to go yet. I haven't even put an ad on Craigslist."

"But I need it now. I'm not coming back here, I mean, I'm leaving town and need it before I leave," said Brian.

The woman shook her head. "I really shouldn't let it go yet."

Brian stood up with the puppy still in his arms. "How about if I take them all?"

When they got in the truck, Brian with a big box of puppies in his lap, Nick laughed. "What are you going to do with six puppies, Brian?"

"Nick, you know you want one. Right?"

Nick coughed. "Um, how did you know that?"

"Just a guess." Brian picked up each puppy one at a time and held it to his face. "How could you not? Look how cute they are!"

"Okay, that accounts for two of the six puppies, what about the other four?"

Brian nodded. "I have plans. I don't think I will have any trouble at all giving away these puppies."

CHAPTER FIFTY-FIVE

RAY HAD BEEN sitting hidden behind a tree—with a perfect view of the house—for days now, and hadn't seen anything except the man and woman who lived there coming and going. Finally, the wagon that he had seen before came into view. When the two men walked from the barn, he recognized one as the man who had been having dinner with Lindy. The other man was the one with the rifle who ran him out of town. His trigger finger felt itchy as he watched them climb into a truck and drive off.

Hours passed before they returned with the truck loaded. As they walked back and forth from the truck to the wagon, Ray reached over, opened the glove compartment, and pulled out his gun. He didn't know who he wanted to kill first, Lindy's boyfriend or the guy who had the rifle. Slowly, he rolled down the window, held the gun up, aimed carefully, and quietly said, "Bang!" Quickly, he realized how stupid that was, pulled the gun back inside the car, and rolled the window up. Ray knew better than to indulge in such stupid fantasy games when there was more at stake. Returning the gun to the glove compartment, he continued watching the two men.

When they entered the house, he was able to relax. But they didn't stay inside long, and when they came out, Ray expected them to go to the wagon, but instead, they climbed back into the truck again and took off. What was that about? What were they up to?

Waiting around for his supplies to arrive was getting tiring. Watching this house all day was even worse. But soon, it wouldn't matter. His supplies would come and everything would work out perfectly. If he only had them now, he could fix her but good. Trap her boyfriend over here while she was there.

Ray didn't totally understand the *arrangement* of the town, but he didn't care, either. One day he had hiked to just above the cave and then walked back toward the ranch house. He had walked until a series of boulders blocked his path, and he never did find one track that might indicate another path to the little town on the other side of the cave. Then on the main trail, he had ridden the motorbike past the turnoff to the cave and never saw one other trail that could lead to the town. He had gone *miles* down the main trail and never saw any other possible entrances.

Maybe he hadn't gone far enough or had missed it, but even if there was another entrance, the cave was the way they always went. So if he removed that entrance, then it would at the very least cause them a big inconvenience. Ray would prefer more vengeance than that, but for now, it would have to do. On the other hand, if it *was* the only entrance, he rubbed his hands together and laughed gleefully. With any luck he could trap Lindy on one side with her boy on the other.

After the two men from the town had left in the truck

again, the man and woman from the house made many trips to the wagon bringing bagfuls of something. He didn't know what it was, and he didn't care. Nothing interested him like revenge.

When the men returned, they briefly entered the house carrying a big box, and then took the box to the wagon. Off they went, with Lindy's boyfriend looking into the box and moving his mouth like he was talking. What a loser! And Lindy was a loser to have chosen him.

The wagon disappeared through the gate, and Ray drove the car to where he had hidden the motorbike. He'd wait a few minutes for them to pass by, and then he would follow the tracks again to make sure he was right about the path. Twenty minutes later, he started the motorbike and drove it slowly down the trail following the fresh tracks. And as expected, they led him to the trail to the cave. After turning around, he rode back to his car and hid the motorbike again.

Stepping into the car, he heard his cell phone ring. It was his buddy from prison. "Yeah. You got it, yet?"—"All right! I was hoping that you wouldn't leave me hanging."—"Naw, you're right, I should have known better."—"Can I come over now to get it?"—"Great. See ya soon. Bye."

Ray pushed the button on the phone and sat back completely satisfied. It would be a long drive, and he wouldn't get back until well after dark, but when he returned, he'd have the dynamite! And with it, he'd blow the cave to kingdom come!

CHAPTER FIFTY-SIX

RACHEL AND LINDY were setting the table when the front door opened. They had been expecting Nick any time, so Lindy didn't think anything of it, until Rachel said, "Hi, Nick. Oh! Hello, Brian!"

Then Lindy turned around and saw him, with a smile on his face, carrying a big box. She smiled at him, nodded, and then returned to the table.

"Boys! I mean, Oscar and Jamie! Come here!" When all three boys came running, Nick said, "Oops. Sorry, Cody."

Brian put the box down, and the boys peered inside. It was Cody who spoke first. "Puppies!"

Lindy walked to the box and peered inside. There were three puppies inside, all with their faces turned up and their tails wagging. The littlest one looked up at Lindy and made eye contact. Her heart melted. Ray would never let her have a dog, and even after he went to prison, she and Cody were too busy getting back on their feet again to think about getting a dog. Oh, how she would love that little one!

"Oscar, Jamie, you two boys decide which puppy you

want. The whole family will share the dog. Okay?"

Oscar looked in the box and backed away. "Jamie can decide. I like them all."

Jamie reached in, petted all the puppies, and then pulled one out. "I like this one." Then he looked up at Nick. "Is he all right, Papa?"

"He's perfect, Jamie. Just perfect." Nick looked at Oscar. "You're awesome!" Oscar smiled and followed Jamie out of the room, both of them petting their new puppy.

Lindy was about to look in the box to see if the smallest puppy was still there, when there was a knock at the door. She took a deep breath and stepped back to the table, straightening up what was already perfectly set.

Nick opened the door and said, "Hello, Kat!"

"Hi, Nick. I heard you had puppies over here!"

"Come on in! There's two left. You can have your pick."

"Hi, Rachel, Lindy, Brian, Cody." She leaned over the box. "What do we have here? Oh, they are cute! The dog is for David, but he sent *me* over here to pick it out for him! The nerve!" She sounded mad, but she had a smile on her face.

Lindy watched her looking into the box, touching both puppies. Cody was watching her, too, with a frown on his face. Clearly, he wanted a puppy, too, but they were guests here. There was no way they could impose any more on Nick and Rachel's kindness. They were imposing enough already just being here.

"I'll take this one, the little girl. When she gets old enough, we'll have to take her *there* to get spayed." Kat stood up holding the puppy up to her face. "Oh, David is going to love you, little girl! Wait till he sees you!" She walked toward the door with the puppy still in front of her face. "Thanks, Nick!"

"Don't thank me, thank Brian. He's the one who dragged six puppies back here!"

"Thanks, Brian. And see you two girls tomorrow, for girls' day out!" Kat slipped out the door.

"Mommy, can't I have a puppy, too?" Cody looked at her with a face so sad, and wetness beginning at the corners of his eyes.

Lindy knelt down beside him and put her hands on his shoulders. "I'm sorry, sweetie, but we're *guests* here. It wouldn't be right." She felt a little angry with Brian tempting Cody like this and making him feel bad.

"Of course it would be," said Nick. "I built a puppy-proof area in the backyard yesterday. It's *two* puppy proof."

"Lindy, I checked with Nick before I brought the puppies over. I know it's the last one, but he's yours if you want him. I hope it's the one you wanted."

Lindy, feeling confused with all the excitement and her own wavering emotions, closed her eyes, leaned over the box, and looked in. Cody stepped up beside her. "Mommy, it's the little one! That's the one I wanted!" Lindy picked it up, kissed it on the top of the head, and then handed it to Cody. "It's the one I wanted, too!"

"Thank you, Brian." She stood on her tiptoes and kissed him on the cheek. "And thank you for the horse. I love her already."

Brian looked surprised. "You saw her?"

Lindy nodded. "I wanted to see what kind of horse you bought me. She's beautiful!"

Brian hugged Lindy tightly. "I have to leave now—gotta get up early tomorrow for guard duty. Do you think we can talk tomorrow after you get back?"

Lindy didn't know what he wanted to talk about, since there had been no resolution with Ray, but whatever it was, she was fine with it, so she nodded. She was so happy right now that she couldn't stand it. Glancing over at the three boys playing with the two puppies, she didn't know when she had ever been happier.

CHAPTER FIFTY-SEVEN

BRIAN WASN'T READY to wake up so early, and he finally admitted to himself that he would be glad when the guard duty assignments were over. Of course, if they were over, that would mean that Ray was gone, and then he and Lindy could be together. So, it was more than just not waking up so early that appealed to him.

The children had complained the night before that they couldn't bring the puppy home with them. But Brian knew it would be too much to handle getting up early and having to deal with a new puppy. He would be safe and secure—and probably feel better, too—with his little brother.

The brother was the puppy that Brian had given to his Ma and Pa. Their old dog had passed on months ago, and they didn't have the heart to get another. But he had seen them petting Jenna's and Josiah's dogs, so Brian had taken it upon himself to get them a puppy. And how his mother beamed when he handed the pup to her! And his father couldn't keep his hands off the puppy. Yes, it was the right decision.

"Pa?" Archie came in rubbing the sleep out of his

eyes. "Do you have to guard again today?"

Brian hugged the child to him. "Yes, Arch. Why?"

"'Cause I think we need to leave," said the boy.

Brian glanced out the window, and the sky was already lightening. "Yup, you're right, my man! Go get yourself dressed, all right? And wake your brother."

Thirty minutes later, they were pulling up in front of the cave, with Amy huddled beside him—she had woken up this time—and the boys riding in the back. Brian yawned, waved at Josiah, and then climbed down off the wagon.

"Hey, Brian. I see you filled the whole town with puppies!" Josiah stood there with his hands on his hips.

Brian nodded. "Yup. I figured the town could use a little excitement—the good kind!"

"I approve. And it's been great for Eliza and Samuel. I didn't realize how much they missed your old dog."

"Would you mind bringing the wagon to town again? Leave the children at the hotel?"

"Sure. No problem." Josiah ran his hand along Dolly's neck and gave her a pat. "We need to get this girl back so she can get fed." Josiah shook his head. "Girls' day out! Whoever heard of such a thing?"

"I think it will be good for Lindy. She needs to get her mind off all the bad things that have happened and all the bad things that can happen. I hope she can relax there."

Josiah attached his horse to the back of the wagon like before. "I've gotta go get some sleep. See ya later, Brian. Hope you have a quiet day." He climbed into the wagon and then turned back to look at Brian. "Oh! It was a quiet night. Nothing happened."

Brian nodded. "That's good. Thanks and bye." He

245

gave each child a quick kiss on the head. "You children be good now. I love you." And the wagon quickly disappeared in the heavy brush.

He sat down on the ground by the entrance to the cave, with his back to the rock. And he started thinking about Lindy. How much he wanted to see her and how much it bothered him to see her. The waiting was killing him. No, not the waiting. It was the unknown.

If he knew that she would marry him in a month, or even a year, he could patiently wait. But not knowing how long it would take—or even if it ever would happen . . . What if Ray left town and they never knew? Would Ray's prolonged absence leave her feeling safe enough to marry him? There was no way to know. Even if he discussed it with Lindy, she might feel differently later. Yes, it was the unknown that was killing him. He sighed deeply and shifted around so a small nodule on the rock wasn't poking into his back.

Then he went over in his mind his trip over *there* the day before. On the way back, the wagon had been so laden down that Dolly could barely get it up the hill. Both Brian and Nick had to get behind and push. It made them laugh. Dolly was grateful, though! And when Brian had finished distributing the puppies, it had taken him and Nick a long time to unpack the wagon. They had stashed most of the forbidden items in Nick's bedroom at the sheriff's office. Brian wouldn't take them home until he had his own home to go to. That was another reason to want the whole guarding job to be done. He'd spend the whole day here instead of working on his house or helping Nick with the improvements on the sheriff's office.

Then Brian thought about everything that he had

bought. The electronics made him smile. He knew the children would love them, and he thought that Lindy would enjoy them, too. After purchasing the six iPads— one for every member of the family—Nick had showed him these little objects that made music. So he bought one of those for everyone, also. And the games and toys for the children—he hadn't even told them about those, because they were too excited about the puppy to care. But he could bring those home soon. And the solar equipment he had bought, including a solar shower. And after trying out a shower at Zack and Madison's house, he was happy about that decision.

When they were at the lumber store buying Nick's doors and some other lumber and more building tools, Brian had seen a fan and asked Nick what it was. Remembering the long, hot nights when he lived in the East, he had bought two of the fans—knowing he would have to use the solar plug-in devices to get them to work. And he bought several flashing—no—flashlights and enough rechargeable batteries to last forever. And of course, the solar battery recharger. And as much as he loved the ice cream from the future, he had decided to buy an ice cream maker so he could make it here. He was going to buy the electric kind and attach it to his solar equipment, but decided on the hand crank kind instead. The whole family could have fun helping to make it. And the solar refrigerator would make Lindy happy. Brian was very happy with all his purchases. And he felt like he didn't *ever* have to go back there. And Lindy didn't have to, either. Unless she wanted to, of course. For a girls' day out!

CHAPTER FIFTY-EIGHT

LINDY FELT ANXIOUS and uneasy about going, but when she and Rachel arrived at the hotel to the festive atmosphere, she felt a lot better. Sarah was already there, and Jenna was giving last minute instructions to Josiah on caring for baby Milo. Although Granny had volunteered to take care of him until Josiah could get some sleep.

"I'll take care of the squalin' brat," she had said, but she held Milo gently in her arms and looked at him with such love that it deeply touched Lindy. It was so pleasurable watching Granny and the infant, that she would have continued until they left if Eliza and Samuel hadn't distracted her.

Eliza had her hand on Samuel's face, and she was looking at him with such intensity that Lindy couldn't tear her eyes away, though she felt that she was intruding on an intimate moment. "You take care of yourself," Eliza said. "And know that I'll always love you—no matter where I am." At that, she broke down and ran out of the hotel to the waiting wagon outside.

"Guess it's time to go. Everybody outside!" said Jenna, herding everyone out.

"All aboard that's coming aboard!" said Ryan.

Eliza stood by the side of the wagon, wiping away her tears. Lindy stepped up to her and whispered, "You don't have to go, Eliza, really, you don't."

Eliza shook her head and said, "Go on. Get in. I'll sit on the outside. Let's get this over with. I can't stand the waiting."

Lindy climbed into the wagon and sat next to Ryan. Then Eliza climbed in. The other women, Rachel, Kat, Jenna, and Sarah, all rode their horses, which were tied to the railing outside the hotel. With one hand on the reins, Ryan raised the other arm straight up and motioned forward. "Wagon ho! Forward march!" And Dolly moved forward, and the horses followed, with the women chattering away—Eliza and Lindy staying silent.

When they arrived at the cave, Brian, who had been sitting on the ground, stood up and bowed. "Morning, ladies. Hallo, Ryan."

"Good morning, Brian!" said all the women in unison, except Lindy and Eliza. Lindy just smiled, and Eliza stared straight ahead with a vacant expression on her face.

"Brian, you keeping the ole Red Bluff safe while we're away?" asked Ryan, encouraging Dolly forward into the cave.

"Sure am, boss. Have a fun day, ladies. You stay safe out there."

He might have said something else, but the women began chattering again, and Lindy missed it. When they exited the cave, Lindy looked around quickly. She didn't know what she expected to see—Ray?—but there was nothing to be seen except surroundings similar to what she had just left. It amazed her the similarities of the place, and yet they were over a hundred years apart. As they bumped down the path toward the main trail, Lindy wondered what Eliza was thinking about. She put her hand on her arm. "You okay, Eliza?" The older woman nodded, but her vacant expression didn't change.

Lindy began thinking about Brian, how handsome he looked today—how handsome he looked every day! And especially handsome riding that big, white horse. She wondered what it would be like to be married to him. Although she knew that it would be nothing like her marriage to Ray, she still wondered what it would feel like. One thing she knew for sure: Brian would make her feel loved. That was something she felt sure about—because he already made her feel that way. Would Ray ever be far enough out of her life that she could feel comfortable living a happy life with Brian? She hoped so.

They came to the gates, went through them—with Jenna unlatching and latching them from the back of her horse—and then Ryan parked the wagon beside the barn. Jenna and Sarah put their horses out in the pasture with the few cows that were out there, and Kat and Rachel put their horses in the barn with Dolly and the two horses that lived there. Then everyone walked to the door and knocked.

Zack opened the door. "Hallo, everyone! I heard you were coming! Listen, Ryan, I talked to Nick and Brian about this yesterday. Would you mind taking several bags of money back, so I don't have to deal with it for a while? Madison and I have finals coming up and—"

"No worries, bud. I'll load them in the wagon when we return."

"If I'm home, I'll help," said Zack.

"Time to rock! Come on, girls!" yelled Jenna. "Let's go

get cinnamon rolls at Donovan's!"

As the women rushed out, Lindy and Eliza followed quietly. Lindy felt bad about Eliza, but didn't think there was anything she could do to help.

Jenna drove to the restaurant, and the six women piled into a booth in the back. Lindy and Eliza had gotten in first, at opposite sides. Lindy was glad she was sitting across from Eliza, so she could at least offer smiles of encouragement. But worrying about Eliza made her realize that she wasn't worried for herself, and she found that interesting.

When the waitress poured the coffee and served the cinnamon rolls, the talk temporarily quieted. Then Sarah said, "Oh, man! These are delicious! I had forgotten how wonderful they are!" And everyone started talking again.

Kat was reserved, though. And after a few minutes she leaned over to Lindy and whispered, "Is Eliza okay today? She looks pale."

Lindy shook her head. "No, she isn't okay. But I think she'll be all right once we get home."

After they left the restaurant, it was a whirlwind of shopping at the mall. They went into every clothing store there was, but mostly came up empty because they didn't carry much that was period appropriate for the nineteenth century. They did better at the thrift stores. Then they had lunch at the Thai restaurant. It was delicious, and Lindy thought that maybe Eliza perked up a little after eating. But it wasn't until they drove past the hotel —the same hotel where she lived in the nineteenth century—that Eliza began feeling better.

Eliza nodded when she saw it. "Yeah, I could live there, couldn't I? That wouldn't be so bad." The only one who heard was Lindy, and she wasn't going to argue. But they'd be home in a couple of hours. Jenna called Ryan on his cell phone, hoping that he would answer, and he did. Ryan needed another hour before he was ready to go, so Jenna cheered.

"What d'ya say, girls? Bowling? We have time for one game!"

They walked in and rented shoes, even Eliza—though when she realized what they wanted her to do, she declined. Lindy did manage to talk her into rolling one ball down the alley, which amounted to a gutter ball, but it made Eliza smile, so Lindy was glad that she had talked her into it. At the end of the game—Lindy got 78, but didn't feel bad because she hadn't played for years—they picked up the penicillin that Kat wanted and headed back to the ranch.

Loading the wagon didn't take long because Ryan had his share already loaded, and he and Zack were just finishing loading the money bags in. All of the women's purchases didn't amount to much, so they were piled on top of everything else. Lindy had bought two more long skirts and several blouses. Then she lucked out when she found some cowboy boots that were her size. Now she was all set for her new life—if only Ray would leave her alone.

After passing through the gates, the wagon and four riders headed toward the cave. Lindy noticed that Eliza leaned a little forward like she was surprised she was returning. Even Lindy was happy to be going back to the nineteenth century, which she had come to love. Of course, a certain handsome cowboy had nothing to do with that. Nope, nothing.

CHAPTER FIFTY-NINE

RAY WAS MAD at himself for not being prepared, but of course he knew it was Lindy's fault, so he wasn't that mad. If it wasn't for her, everything would be in place. The morning had started with him waking sore and stiff on the floor of his buddy's apartment. And after a night of drinking, he had a raging headache. That was Lindy's fault, too. If she hadn't sent him to prison, he wouldn't have met someone who forced him to get drunk when he didn't really want to.

Luckily, he had woken up early. But it had taken a while to drive back to Red Bluff, and by the time he swung by to look at the ranch house, he saw that wagon parked at the barn again. Although he waited half an hour, no one came out, and then he noticed that two of the vehicles were missing. Cursing himself for not noticing that before, he had to hit the dashboard several times to calm himself down. He couldn't take the chance of driving recklessly and getting arrested.

Then, as long as he had missed them, he drove to Donovan's to have a late breakfast at their drive-thru. And who should be walking out of there as he pulled into the lot, but Lindy and a bunch of other women. Ray wanted immediately to go and set off the dynamite, but his headache was so bad that he knew he needed to eat. What was one more hour, anyway? The women looked like they were going to make a day of it.

Still, he wanted to get it done, so he hurried through breakfast and got back to where he was staying as quickly as he could. He carefully wrapped the dynamite in an old pair of jeans and placed it into the backpack. Ray didn't want it going off while he rode the motorbike to the cave! After placing the backpack by the door, he decided to just lie down for a few minutes to rest. The big meal made him sleepy. So he laid down on his bed and closed his eyes.

Three hours later, Ray woke up with a start. Disoriented, he looked around the room wondering where the bars were. Then he realized. It had been another dream of still being in prison. They always made him wake up looking for bars. When he glanced at the clock, he began cursing himself. "If I missed an opportunity to get that broad—!" Then he quickly got up, grabbed the backpack and drove past the ranch house, just to be sure. No, he got lucky. The wagon was still there.

After driving to where the motorbike was, he put on the backpack, started up the bike, hopped on, and drove slowly to the turnoff to the cave. He hid the motorbike in the bushes and hiked up the hill. After placing the dynamite carefully on the ledge inside the cave, he reached in his pocket for his cigarette lighter and found it missing. Shaking his head, he hit himself in the jaw. "That'll teach you to be so stupid!" he grumbled.

Then he began searching his other pockets for matches and smiled when he found a book in his back pocket.

Opening it up, he saw two matches. Since he only needed one to light the sticks, he didn't care. When he lit the first one, a gust of wind blew it out before he even had a chance to get it close to the fuse. For the second one, he put his body between the cave entrance and the dynamite. Then he struck the match, gave it a second to go steady, and then with excitement building, he held the match to the first fuse. It wouldn't catch! So he held what was left of the match to the second fuse, and it wouldn't catch, either! Did that jerk give me defective dynamite, he wondered. No, he swore it was good stuff.

Ray realized that he had to go get his lighter, so he turned around to leave the cave, but felt angry that his plans weren't going smoothly. "You stupid—!" he yelled.

"What? Who's there?"

It was a voice from the other side of the cave. Ray grabbed the dynamite, ran out of the cave and up the hill a few feet, and hid behind some thick brush where he could still see the cave entrance. Then he waited.

A minute later, he saw a rifle poking out from the cave. "Anyone here?" It was the man who Lindy had had dinner with. In a moment of rage, Ray reached behind him for his gun, but he had left that behind, too. The man looked around, but when he didn't see anything, he walked back in to the cave. Ray waited a full ten minutes to make sure the coast was clear before stepping gingerly out. He wrapped the dynamite up inside the backpack and left it where he had been hiding. Quietly, he walked by the cave and glanced inside.

What he saw disturbed him. The ledge, where the dynamite would go, was a lot closer to his side of the cave than the other side. And there was that bend in the cave, too. The dynamite would still do its job, but maybe

255

too well. Ray decided that what he needed to do was fix the trail so the motorbike could make it to the cave. He could walk it up, so lover-boy wouldn't hear it. Then he could park it outside the cave so he could take off right after lighting the fuses. It wouldn't matter if they could hear it then or not. After all, that would be safer. Safety first, laughed Ray to himself.

Slowly, he worked his way down the hill, moving rocks as he went. When he finished, he looked back at his handiwork. There was a path that he could get the motorbike up without too much trouble. Perfect! Now he had to get back, get the lighter, and return to finish the job. He walked the motorbike down the main trail far enough that he didn't think anyone on the other side of the cave could hear it. Then he raced back to where his car was. Maybe he had a lighter there.

When Ray got to the car and found the lighter, he felt grateful that he didn't have to go all the way back to his place. Because he was sure that he would have missed the opportunity to blow up the cave with Lindy on this side and *her* kid on the other side. He raced back along the path and just in case, turned off the engine well before the cut-off trail up to the cave. Walking the motorbike along, Ray felt his blood coursing through his veins. Finally! Revenge would be his, and they wouldn't even know what hit them. Or who.

Turning the front wheel, he headed up the hill, but with no momentum, he struggled getting the motorbike up to the cave. After laying it down several times to move more rocks or to smooth out the uneven earth, he kicked the bike—silently, he didn't want anyone to hear—and continued up the hill. It took him much longer than he had anticipated, but finally he reached the entrance to the cave. Pushing down the kickstand, Ray sat down on a nearby rock to catch his breath.

Still huffing and puffing, but eager to get going, he retrieved the backpack and carefully took out the dynamite. Then he tiptoed into the cave, set it on the ledge, and fished his lighter out of his pocket. His breathing had returned to normal now, and as he was about to flick the lighter on, he stopped and listened. Voices? He took a couple silent steps farther into the cave. No, not coming from there. Then he stepped closer to the entrance of the cave. Yes, definitely there. If they saw the motorbike, they would know! He raced outside and pushed the motorbike behind the brush where he had hidden it before. Then he rushed back into the cave as quietly as he could and removed the dynamite. Taking it with him behind the brush, he waited.

The voices got louder and louder, and then he heard the clip-clop of a horse's hooves on rock. Ray knew he had hidden none too soon. If he had waited any longer, they would have caught him. Although he was nervous about what almost happened, a big smile spread across Ray's face. As the wagon came into view, followed by several horses, Ray looked at Lindy sitting in the front seat and said to himself, "Take a long last look at this side of the cave, because you ain't ever going to see it again!" Then he nodded, satisfied with himself as he watched the wagon disappear into the cave. It didn't work out exactly the way he wanted—to have Lindy on one side and the boy on the other—but still, it would be good to block their usual route. He wasn't going to back down now, regardless. And maybe, if he worked really quickly, he could catch them still in the cave and blow them to bits!

Listening carefully, he walked slowly to the entrance of the cave and watched as the last of the riders disappeared around the bend. Then he hurried over to the motorbike and parked it in front of the cave entrance. Grabbing the dynamite, he quickly set it up on the ledge. He flicked the lighter, but it didn't start. After two more tries, it finally did. Smiling from ear to ear, he lit one fuse and then the other. Casually, because he wanted the moment to last as long as it could, he walked out of the cave and swung his leg over the motorbike. He kicked the starter, but it didn't start. Kicking it again frantically, it still wouldn't start. Ray turned around to look into the cave, and the last thing he ever saw was the explosion and large rocks coming straight for him.

CHAPTER SIXTY

THEY HAD ALL been talking, so nobody heard anything until the explosion roared out of the cave. Dolly, bless her heart, heard something, though, because she pulled the reins out of Ryan's hand and trotted away seconds before the blast. The other horses, who had been behind the wagon, spooked at either the same thing or because of Dolly's quick movements, so nobody was in front of the cave when it happened. Brian had been at the front of the wagon talking to Lindy, luckily, or he might have gotten caught by the force that exploded out of the cave.

Before the dust even settled, Ryan handed the reins to Lindy, and climbed off the wagon. "Everybody okay?" When he heard everyone's assent and didn't see any injuries, he walked toward the cave. "Come on, Brian, let's take a look."

Large rocks had tumbled out of the cave and were now strewn in front of it. Ryan climbed over them and peered into the cave, while Brian hung back, watching. "Completely blocked," said Ryan, shaking his head. "With huge rocks, one as big as a volkswagon. The only way we'll move that thing is with a bulldozer—which is on the other side." Ryan turned around and looked at Brian. "You're smiling—?"

Seeing Ryan's odd expression at his happiness, he said, "Ah, nervous habit." And forced the smile from his lips. Before he did or said anything else, he wanted to see everyone else's reaction to what Ryan obviously considered a catastrophe.

The two men walked over to the front of the wagon, where the horses and riders were. The riders were all shaking their heads.

"No more well-baby checks," said Jenna.

"Thank goodness I have all this penicillin," said Kat, patting her fat saddlebags that were full of the stuff, whatever it was.

"No more frozen pizza," said Rachel. "And just after Nick brought home a solar refrigerator for us."

Ryan spoke up next. "No more special orders. No more trips there to pick up stuff. No more fresh vegetables in the winter." He shook his head. "Thank goodness Zack gave us all that money, though we probably won't need it."

"You know, I'm okay with this. The only thing that I'll miss is getting the newest iPhone," said Sarah. That made everyone laugh and broke the tension.

Eliza didn't seem at all fazed by the blast. She looked relieved. "I have to be honest. I don't mind this at all. I am very grateful that y'all are here and that Jenna helped bring back my boy"—she smiled at Brian—"but I think this is good. If that Ray found his way here, other bad people from the future could find us, too. This is all around better. And I don't think I'm the only one who thinks this is a good thing."

Eliza looked over at Lindy, but as soon as he heard his

mother's words, Brian had reached his arms up toward Lindy. She fell into them, and they kissed, a long, satisfying kiss, as everyone watched, and as time passed, laughed. When they came up for air, Brian, with a giant smile on his face and Lindy still secure in his arms, said, "There's going to be a wedding!"

EPILOGUE

Thanksgiving 1871

Everyone sat around the big table inside the restaurant, which was closed. Josiah sat at the head of the table. The children all sat at the "children's table" a few feet from the adults. They talked quietly among themselves. Josiah cleared his throat.

"Before we serve the turkey, I think we should all go around the room and say what we're grateful for. There have been a lot of changes here, lately, and I, for one, think that it would be a good idea."

"Hear! Hear!" said Samuel. "I agree. Josiah, you go first."

"I am grateful that a certain cave brought this woman"—he put his arm around Jenna—"into my life. And I'm grateful for the birth of our healthy son"—he glanced beside him to the boy who was sitting in a high

263

chair—"Milo."

Jenna spoke up. "I could not be more grateful for getting caught in a snowstorm that led me to the cave and my new life with my husband." She put her head on Josiah's shoulder.

Matthew put his arm around his wife Sarah. "I am grateful that this woman came into my saloon wanting to sing. I have enjoyed her singing ever since, and I am forever grateful that she agreed to marry me."

Sarah looked at him and raised her eyebrows. "I believe that you consented to marry me, partner." Everyone laughed. "I'm grateful that Jenna found the cave so I could work the job of my dreams, and marry the man of my dreams." She kissed Matthew on the cheek, and shrugged. "I miss things in on the other side of the cave, but I always have my solar iPhone charger!"

"I'm glad this woman came into my life," said Doc, with one arm around Kat. "And I don't mind all the new technologies that she brought into my life!"

"Like this!" Kat held up a round device with wires trailing from it.

"What's that?" Edward asked.

"That is a pacemaker for Granny, when the one she has wears out. And I have several more at home. I am grateful that I brought several home a few months ago, *and* that Doc and I had learned how to insert them from Granny's cardiologist."

"Woo hoo!" called Edward. "My bride will stick around to annoy me for more years!"

"What I'm grateful about is that I stopped thinking that David—Doc to you all—was a stupid nineteenth century man and realized how incredibly wonderful he is."

"Of course I am!" said David.

"Oh, one more thing. Zack and Madison obviously weren't able to be here tonight."

"I really do miss my great-granddaughter, but she and Zack are very happy living where—when—they do, and they would not be happy here, anyway." Granny held up her glass. "But here's to Zack and Madison. We love them and miss them!" Everyone held up their glasses toasting Zack and Madison.

"I will be forever grateful to Henry Ralston for moving away and selling me Ralston General Store. And I'm even more grateful that I am married to Mary Elizabeth —the woman I fell head over heels in love with," said Ryan, looking at her with love in his eyes.

"And I will forever be grateful that Ryan came through the cave and into my life," said Mary Elizabeth.

"I speak for Cora and myself"—Cora, sitting next to John Mills nodded—"that we are grateful that the cave brought so many wonderful people into this town."

"Well, I'm grateful that I decided to leave my job in the new Red Bluff to become the sheriff here. And I'm also grateful"—he put his arm around Rachel—"that she agreed to be my wife."

"And I'm grateful," Rachel said, "that Annie, the previous schoolmarm married Henry Ralston so that I could take her job! And I'm very grateful for my husband, Nick, who I'd probably never have been with if we both hadn't moved here!"

Samuel stood up with his glass in his hand. "I am so grateful that Jenna came through that cave to our town, and then found out that our son, Brian, was alive. We will always be grateful to you for that, Jenna." He choked a little, holding back tears, and sat down.

Eliza hesitated before speaking. "If Jenna hadn't come through that cave, our son Brian"—she put her hand on Brian's arm—would not be here with us now. Like Samuel said, Jenna, we will always be grateful to you for helping us to bring him home." Tears ran down her face, and she didn't bother to wipe them away.

"And I'm grateful that Ma and Pa brought me home so that I could meet this woman who means so much to me," Brian put his hand on Lindy's arm and looked at her lovingly. "And I am grateful to be home and here with all of you tonight."

"I'm grateful to be here and be married to this wonderful man who keeps me safe," said Lindy.

"I'm grateful that when Jenna moved here, she brought her sassy, old grandmother with her, so that I could have someone to pester," said Edward, smiling, with his arm around Granny.

"And I'm grateful to have an old codger like you to love!" said Granny. Then she stood up and held up her glass. "And I'm *really* grateful that the dratted cave is no more!"

"Here here!" said Eliza. "I agree!"

"After all," continued Granny, "we have each other, and that's what's really important, right?"

Everyone held up their glasses and agreed, and they had many more happy Thanksgivings to come.